Penelope and Priscilla

and the

Enchanted House of Whispers

Story and Illustrations
by
Jennifer Troulis

Twin Monkeys Press

Penelope and Priscilla and the Enchanted House of Whispers
Second Edition

Cover drawing by Jennifer Troulis

Published 2004 by
Twin Monkeys Press
146 First Street
Dunellen, New Jersey 08812

www.TwinMonkeysPress.com
Whispers@TwinMonkeysPress.com

ISBN: 0-9768602-0-1

Edited by Mary Ellen Lewczyk
Cover Art by Jennifer Troulis
Desktop Publishing by McCartney Media

DEDICATION

For my husband Jim and my children Justin and Samantha—Thank you
for supporting my creative ventures over the years, for believing in me
and for eating lots of leftovers without complaint. Your love inspires me.

I also dedicate this book to the memory of three special women
in my life:

Mary Kozak
Martha Lewczyk
Marie Troulis

ACKNOWLEDGEMENTS

Mom, when I was a little girl, you taught me the importance of a woman's independence. As the years passed, your words endured like a faithful companion, pushing me forward and guiding me. Thank you for all your hard work on the book, for always supporting me, and for being my best friend.

Jo-Ann and Michael Faulkner—Thank you for your friendship, endless encouragement, support, and help with the book and with all of my endeavors. When I felt discouraged, you reminded me of how far I had come and how much further I could go.

Jo-Ann—You put so much time into the early editing of the manuscript. Thank you for both helping and teaching me.

Bill Robins—Thank you for sharing your knowledge with me. I will never forget all of your advice, encouragement, and help with regard to both my writing and the book.

Barbara Gates—Thank you for your friendship and advice early on with regard to my writing.

Erin Brady—Thank you for being the first to love my book. Your positive feedback and enthusiasm for the book means more to me than I could ever express.

Brian Ford—Thank you for helping me to learn not to be afraid.

And, lastly, I would like to thank a very special person, **David McCartney**. Without the use of your equipment, your know-how, and the generous donation of your time, this book would not be possible.

CONTENTS

FOREWARD

I can think of few greater gifts than taking a child on a fantastic journey during which they will not only be entertained, but will hopefully learn something about life and, possibly, themselves. Like many of the great fantasy novels that have gone before, the story of pre-teen, identical twin sisters, Penelope and Priscilla, take the reader on a journey to a wonderfully different world. In the book, mystical talking creatures, an old magical book, and a whispering house help the at-odds sisters come together to protect their family secret.

Along with its subtle emphasis on such timeless values as family unity, friendship, and respect, the book deals with important issues in a child's life such as the loss of a parent, moving to a new town, and the need for peer acceptance. I believe the growth process that both Penelope and Priscilla experience, illustrates important ideas. The most prominent belief is that strength and self-confidence will help to achieve any goal.

This, my first book, was originally inspired by and written for my two children, who very early-on loved books about magic. I also felt there weren't enough books whose main characters were twins. Later, after the book was finished, I realized how much I loved to write. I also realized the endless creative possibilities that writing offered, and I could not wait to touch the lives of children everywhere.

Chapter One

Priscilla Moves to Dunville

On the first night in her new home, Priscilla Post listened to the rain as she lay awake in her bed with her sapphire blue eyes closed. Like long brittle fingernails, it *tap, tap, tapped* on the fragile old glass of her bedroom window. Unable to sleep, she wondered what would happen to her family if the people in this town didn't accept them.

With her favorite teddy bear, Ashford, held tightly against her chest, she began talking to the darkness that covered her like a second skin.

"I need help! Things between Penelope and me aren't the way they used to be. Just yesterday I asked her to show me how to make a new braid, something she used to love to do, and she said she was too busy. That's what she always says lately. I feel like I'm losing her. And this town . . . I don't know what's wrong with the people of this town, but it isn't helping matters. I just want to feel like a family again. I just want to have a real home again," she said as tears formed in her eyes.

As she reached over to her nightstand for a tissue, she brushed her long sandy blond hair behind her ears and turned on the light. Lying back against her pillow, she noticed the old maple tree outside her window. Silhouetted against the flashes of lightening, its leaves were rustling fiercely as if engaged in a wild dance. A moment later, a loud clap of thunder erupted somewhere in the distance, causing the old walls of the house to shake and its windows to rattle. Priscilla pulled her long skinny legs up to her chest. Storms had never frightened her before, but this time it was different. *It must be this house*, she thought. *Those old leaky windows practically invite the storm in, and the walls . . . they seem to magnify every sound.* Trembling, she held onto Ashford even more tightly and pulled her covers up over her nose. From under the covers, she chanted, "Make it stop . . . make it stop . . . make it stop."

Suddenly, all was quiet. Even the rain and wind had stopped. Priscilla was pleased with herself. For a second, she felt that the forces of nature had obeyed her request.

She turned out her light, once again finding herself in total darkness. Moments later, on the verge of sleep, she heard a faint voice. It seemed to come from within the walls of the house and wrapped around her like a gentle hug.

"I'll be your family," the voice whispered.

Unsure of what she heard, she sat up and called out, "Who's there? Is anybody there?"

When no one answered, she dropped back onto her pillow and fell fast asleep.

The following morning, Priscilla knelt on her mom's favorite green velvet sofa in the parlor. She had watched the rain fall for over an hour and was getting restless. She leaned in towards the large window before her and pressed her nose up against the rippled antique glass and inspected her new neighborhood.

As she watched the raindrops fall to the soggy ground where they gathered in large pools, she wondered what they were doing here. Maybe this dismal country weather was causing her to be depressed—or, perhaps it was that she had been torn away from the home where she spent the last 12 years of her life.

She took off her orange baseball cap and scratched her head. *Everything happened so fast. It's hard to believe that yesterday I was surrounded by everything familiar; and today, I'm in a strange town where I don't know anyone. And, to make matters worse, our neighbors seem odd,* she thought as she adjusted her pigtails.

From overhead, thunder roared. The furious sound forced its way through the delicate plaster walls of the old house and caused Priscilla to tremble. She remembered the voice that she heard the night before. It seemed to have come after the storm had passed. She wondered if the same would be true on this day. A few seconds later—although it felt much longer—the furious noise dissolved into the air around her. She was relieved, but still tense. She knew that the thunder would be back. For a moment, she closed her eyes.

"**Smash!**" The sound of glass shattering in the kitchen startled her.

"**Mom . . . are you okay?**" she yelled.

Mom answered in a tone that Priscilla had not heard in a long time—she sounded happy again. "**Don't worry honey—I'm okay. It wasn't the good stuff.**"

Priscilla was starting to feel guilty for leaving her mother to unpack by herself. *Ever since we sold our old house,*

Mom has seemed so stressed. I guess the least I could do is help her put things away.

"**I'm coming to help**," she called.

On her way to the kitchen, she glanced over at her sister, Penelope, who had been lying on the floor next to the sofa. She had been reading a book for what seemed like hours. Priscilla could feel some small pieces of toast and scrambled eggs from breakfast rise up into her throat.

"Why wasn't *she* helping to unpack?" she asked herself.

But, it had been a long time since Penelope did anything for anyone else. When their dad died a year earlier, she blamed Priscilla for her not being there to say goodbye to him.

I know Penelope's had a hard time over the past year, but what about me? Thing's haven't been easy for me either, Priscilla thought angrily.

Penelope was Priscilla's identical twin and her best friend. From birth, the two had a bond that seemed to surpass their sibling status. Everyone who knew the girls, and even those who didn't know them well, knew what they were about just by looking at them. It was as if each wore a neon sign: one reading, "I am very girly" and the other reading, "I have no interest whatsoever in being girly."

At the age of two and a half, Penelope showed her independence by insisting on picking out her own clothes and dressing herself each morning. Dresses in soft pastel colors were her favorite outfits. She would not wear a pair of pants without putting up a fight.

When she turned five, glittery high-heeled shoes and bright, funky colors dominated her wardrobe and captured the attention she so desired. At school, parents and teachers alike seemed to watch for her each morning in the schoolyard to see what she was wearing. As she passed through the front doors, she would kiss her mother, smile, and wave to all of the other parents. On several occasions she loudly wished everyone a "*Good Day*".

Mom once said, "Penelope has a personality to match her clothes—loud and commanding."

From the same age, it was clear that Priscilla would take a different path—one littered with toy trucks, baseball mitts, and an insect collection that changed each time she discovered a new type of bug. She didn't care much about clothes—an old, comfortable tee shirt and jeans were her favorites—or competing with the other girls at school over who had the newest and coolest toys on the market. When she turned eight, she gave up on hanging around with the girls in her class all together. Beside her sister, her best friend was a boy named Jefferson Tate. He was the captain of the boy's basketball team and could spit further than anyone she knew. She, Jefferson and some other members of the boy's basketball team got together every Wednesday after school and played in the park until dark.

Penelope let her sister know how she felt about her relationship with boys.

"The kids are talking . . . don't you care about what people are saying?" she would ask.

Priscilla's response was always the same. "No—and you shouldn't either."

But the truth was that Penelope did. She let the opinions of other's dictate how she felt about herself.

Unlike her sister, Priscilla wasn't influenced by other kid's opinions. She didn't care if it wasn't cool to collect bugs and to play ball with the guys. She believed that by being her own person, she would eventually be recognized and rewarded with something that she too desired—popularity and a sense of belonging.

The amazing thing about the girl's relationship was that no matter what their differences were, they all simply melted away when they were together. Some called it *the magic of sisterhood.* Others said that the love and energy that their family possessed held them all together like glue.

Tears began to well up in Priscilla's eyes. She wished that all it took was glue to fix things, but she knew no one could change what happened in the past. *If I could go back in time, I would have insisted that Penelope stay home to help Mom and me take care of Dad. Instead, I talked her into going to that stupid dance. I wish she had never listened to me.*

Priscilla had apologized to Penelope a zillion times in the past. Things were better between them for a while, but after Mom told them they were moving, she seemed angry with Priscilla again. *If only she had been there to say goodbye to Dad like I had been, everything would be different now . . . I'm sure of it.*

From time to time, Priscilla complained to her mother about her sister's attitude, and Mom's reply was always the same: "We have to be patient with her. She'll come around."

But Priscilla didn't think she could wait. For a year, she had been without her chess partner, her confidant, and her best friend. Now, living in a new town, she really needed a friend.

Outside the kitchen door, Priscilla ran into her mother.

"I thought that you were coming in," Mom said as she
wiped her hands on a pink dishtowel.

"I guess I was taking my time."

"That's okay . . . I wanted to talk to the two of you
anyway."

"As we were coming into town yesterday, I saw a
couple of cute shops. How would you girls like to go into
town later and look around?"

Penelope looked up and smiled. "Sure Mom—that
sounds good. Maybe we can look for a shoe store."

Turning around, Mom asked, "How does that sound,
Priscilla?"

Priscilla straightened up and grabbed her stomach.
The mere idea of going into town for any reason made her
queasy. But, knowing that protesting would do no good, she
agreed. As she followed her mother to the kitchen, she
thought about her new neighbors and the bizarre welcome
her family received the day before.

The drive from the city was a long one. When they
arrived in Dunville, Mrs. Post cautiously made a left onto
Lincoln Avenue, which ran through the center of town, and
then made a right onto Jackson Street. The rain was pouring
down and the streets were slick.

"Jackson Street . . . I like the sound of that," Priscilla
said as she mused at the fact that the huge old trees that lined
Jackson Street on both sides looked like soldiers standing at
attention. "The homes around here are so beautiful!"

Priscilla secretly wished that their house looked as
beautiful as the rest of the houses in town.

The town of Dunville was known for its exuberantly-colored, immaculately-kept, old colonial and Victorian-style homes.

"Why are you talking like you've never been here before?" Penelope asked.

"Well, the last time we were here, I didn't pay much attention."

House after house whizzed by as Mom's beat up, blue, 1989 station wagon darted down the street toward its destination.

"If you remember, our house is down the road a couple of miles," Mom said excitedly.

Priscilla had been fumbling with the tattered baseball mitt on her lap until her attention shifted to a huge white colonial-style house in the distance. As they moved closer to the pristine house, she noticed something peculiar.

"Hey, guys—look!" she said.

Mom slowed her speed, and Penelope slid over next to Priscilla and peered out the window.

"It's some of our new neighbors," Penelope said. "Why are they just standing there in the pouring rain? Don't they care that they're getting wet? They're going to ruin their clothes!"

Priscilla gave her sister a curious look. *I don't know why, but I'm starting to feel uneasy about this town*, she thought to herself.

Penelope's mouth hung open as their car reached the three neatly dressed men who, she could now see, were performing various forms of yard work. The eldest man was attempting to mow the wet grass. Tall and slender, he had ink black hair and pasty skin that contrasted sharply with his navy blue dress shirt and black slacks.

"What's wrong with this guy?" cried Penelope.

Priscilla felt relieved to know that someone else shared her concern.

"A white dress shirt would have made a bolder statement," Penelope said, pointing to the man with ink black hair.

The other two men were wearing black overalls and white dress shirts. "Well, at least they got the dress shirt thing right," she announced, smiling.

Although annoyed, she wasn't completely surprised by Penelope's response. However, she did expect to hear her mother voice her reaction, but she wasn't paying attention. She had been fiddling with the radio dial for most of the ride.

"**Hey, Mom!**" Priscilla shouted. "Look out the window. I see some of our new neighbors."

Mom glanced up. "Oh! My goodness! They sure do things differently out here in the country."

Priscilla could not believe her ears. Why was she the only one who could see that something was not right here?

"Is the wrong shirt the only strange thing that you noticed?" she asked, turning to her sister.

"What else was I *supposed* to notice?"

Becoming angry, Priscilla tapped her finger on the window. "Look at them! Don't you think it's weird for men who are dressed in their good clothes to be doing lawn chores in the rain? And, their hands aren't even dirty!"

Looking up at the rear view mirror, she could see the surprised expression on her mother's face.

"What's gotten into *you* all of a sudden?" Penelope asked, moving away from her sister.

Priscilla did not answer, but stared out the window.

As their car passed the beautiful old colonial house, Priscilla turned around in her seat and looked out the back window. The men had stopped working and were now standing on the sidewalk, staring after them.

"Mom—did you see how those men looked at us?" she asked, her heart racing.

"No—I didn't. What's wrong now?"

"The look in their eyes . . . I don't know . . . it was just so cold."

"Well, I'm sure that the look wasn't intended for us. They must be cold and feeling miserable from working out in the rain."

"Then why don't they just go inside their houses?" Penelope asked as she opened her purse, took out a small silver mirror, and put on a fresh layer of lip gloss.

As Mom continued down the long stretch of road towards their new house, the rain started to let up. Priscilla noticed several women and children outside. *They are all so nicely dressed,* she thought as she glanced down at her ripped jean shorts and faded team jersey. *I hope they don't always dress that way. Penelope and Mom might fit in, but I sure won't.*

Mom slowed her speed to a crawl, and Priscilla noticed another small group of women and children staring at them. A little further down they passed a few more neighbors who watched them go by. The look in their eyes was always the same—bitter and un-welcoming. *I don't care what Mom says, the problem with these people has nothing to do with the weather.*

"There it is—up ahead," Mom announced, pointing to a large rundown Victorian-style home.

Priscilla felt her stomach begin to churn. She couldn't keep her feelings to herself. She had to say something. "I don't know about you guys, but I feel very unwelcome here," she said in a voice just above a whisper.

At that moment, the air inside the car became very heavy. Although no one said a word, Priscilla could see her mother's expression in the rear view mirror. Her eyes, though looking forward, were wide open and her lips were puckered. Priscilla knew that her mother was annoyed.

"Good heavens, Priscilla—do you always have to be so doom and gloom? We just got here. You haven't met any of the neighbors, yet you've already decided *not* to give them a chance," Mom said finally.

"Mom's right, Priscilla—you're always so negative," Penelope added, in a superior tone.

A few seconds later, Mom pulled into their driveway. When the car came to a stop with a loud *HISS*, Priscilla opened her door and jumped out. "That was a long drive—my leg was starting to fall asleep," she said, jumping up and down.

Mom and Penelope stayed in the car and appeared to be checking their hair and make-up. When they finally got out, Mom hurried to the back of the car, opened the door, and began grabbing boxes.

"Here—take this," Mom said, handing Priscilla a large cardboard box containing Priscilla's cherished baseball collection.

"Thanks," she said as she accepted the box, cradled it in her arms, and headed towards the house. A moment later, the bottom of the box fell out and baseballs of different colors and sizes rolled in every direction. "**Darn!**"

Mom put down her box to help but, before she could grab a single ball, Penelope called her into the house.

"I'm sorry, Priscilla, I have to see what she wants. You *know* how Penelope gets when she can't find something," Mom said, standing up.

"It's okay, I can handle this," Priscilla said as she continued to gather up the balls.

As she knelt down to pick up the last ball, she smelled something putrid coming from the direction of the street. Her first thought was *burnt oranges*! When she looked across the street, a bright red baseball cap caught her eye. To her surprise, the cap was perched on the head of an old woman smoking a pipe—*could she really be smoking oranges?* Priscilla wondered. "I've seen many strange things living in the city, but none as strange as this."

The old woman's hair was the color of dusty cotton and she held an ebony pipe to one side of her mouth. She was wearing a faded green plaid dress and dirty white tennis shoes, and her dark eyes were fixed in a trance-like stare on Priscilla. Uncomfortable under her gaze, Priscilla turned away. There was something about the old woman's eyes that frightened her.

After a moment, it came to her—the woman's eyes were empty. There was no sparkle, no hint of emotion, no anything. She had never seen a dead person, but she thought that maybe this is how their eyes would look. This sent a cold shiver down her spine.

"She's worse than our other neighbors," she murmured to herself.

"Come on Priscilla—we have a lot of work to do!" Mom called as she returned from the house.

Priscilla slowly headed back to the car.

"Is everything okay?" Mom asked as she came down the driveway. "You look a little pale."

Priscilla glanced back over her shoulder and saw that the woman was gone. "I'm all right . . . just a little tired I guess."

Mom smiled in a way that told Priscilla that she knew how she felt, and she handed her a new box.

Twenty minutes later, Priscilla reached into the back of the car and pulled out the last box. As she turned around, she was startled. On the driveway, next to her, stood a tiny stranger who looked to be as tall as Grandma's rag mop. The figure looked mysterious, as it was dressed in a long black flowing cape and hood and leaned on a wooden walking stick. At first, Priscilla could not tell if it was a man or a woman.

"It must be an old woman," she said to herself as she noticed the figure's small gnarled hands. "Can I help you?" she asked

"No—but I may be able to help you sometime," the old woman replied, removing her hood.

Priscilla was surprised to see the kindest face and the sweetest smile that she had ever seen. Excited to meet a friendly neighbor she called, "Mom, there's someone . . . "

When she turned back around, the woman was hobbling down the sidewalk.

"Bye!" she shouted as she watched the fringe on the woman's cape brush the ground like flames dancing along a burning log.

A moment later, Penelope strolled out the front door holding a Styrofoam cup. "What are you yelling about?" she snapped. "Can't you see that the neighbors are staring at you?"

Priscilla could not believe her ears. "They're not staring at *me*, they're staring at *us*. If you were paying attention, you would have noticed them earlier."

Penelope did not say another word, but tossed her hair over her shoulder and took another sip from her cup.

"It's useless," Priscilla said to herself as she climbed the porch steps. "Why can't anyone else see what I see—the zombie-like expressions on the neighbor's faces. Why am I the only one who sees that the people in this town greet us with death-like silence and intense glares? Their icy stares go right through me and I feel cold inside."

Before going into the house, she glanced over her shoulder one last time and muttered, "This place gives me the creeps."

A loud clap of thunder brought Priscilla back to the present.

"Priscilla—are you going to just stand there staring off into space?" Mom asked, holding out a box of dishes.

Priscilla quietly accepted the box, began removing the dishes, and started to stack them in the freshly lined cabinets. A half-hour later she was finished unpacking and needed another break. As she headed back into the parlor, she wondered if her sister would still be there. As it turned out, she was laying in the same spot, engrossed in a book titled, *How to Properly Accessorize and Compliment Any Wardrobe.*

"Good book?" Priscilla asked.

When her sister didn't respond, she decided to say something to get her attention. "Hey Penelope—I overheard one of the neighbors say that he thought your shoes were tacky."

Priscilla's plan worked. Penelope sprang up from the floor and glared at her. Her eyes, which were usually the color of perfect sapphires, looked like black marbles. "What did you say?" she replied, her nostrils flaring.

Priscilla started to giggle. "I was only kidding—the neighbors haven't said *boo* to us yet. I just wanted to know what you thought about Dunville so far."

Penelope smoothed her pink cotton dress. "Darn! I'm all wrinkled."

Priscilla watched as her sister headed over to where Mom had hung Grandma Post's antique gilded mirror.

"The people around here are definitely not like the people in the city. Maybe it's all the fresh air or something," Penelope finally replied.

"Are you kidding? It's more than the fresh air. Something is wrong with the people in this town—they don't like us," Priscilla said as she joined her sister in the foyer. "Aren't you the least bit curious why?"

"How can I be curious about something that I don't believe?" Penelope said as she straightened her pink velvet hair ribbon and headed back into the parlor.

Then, with the grace and speed of a baby gazelle, she snatched up her book, turned, and headed upstairs.

Chapter Two

Penelope Changes Her Mind

*T*he next morning, Penelope awoke to the feeling of warm sun on her face. As she opened her eyes, she wondered for just a second if she was dreaming.

It's amazing how the sun adds life to these old walls, she thought as she stretched her arms over her head and yawned.

Painted one shade softer than the color of ripe bananas, the room was now alive. As the rays of the morning sun flowed through the room's two large windows, she smiled, sat up, and then slid to the floor. She wanted so badly to smell the summer air. Sleepily, she walked over to one of the windows, unfastened the lock, and pushed up. Nothing happened. The window had been painted shut.

"It's a beautiful day and I can't enjoy it," she whined to herself.

After beating and pushing on the window, it finally opened with a *bang*.

The warm, fresh air wafted in, gently blowing her purple satin and lace nightgown. She took a deep breath. Today, the air smelled different—clean, sweet, and light.

Gazing out the window towards the neighbor's rose garden, she felt for the first time in months that everything was going to be all right. It was strange, but the move, the house, and even this town now seemed tolerable.

She also began to think about her family's strange trip into town the night before. Not a single person said hello to them, and the rude woman in the dress shop wouldn't let her try on a single dress. But, today, she did not care. Yesterday's problems and worries had vanished with the rain.

Leaving the window open, she drifted back to her bed like a cloud on a breeze. She grabbed her favorite porcelain doll, Emily, closed her eyes, and fell back onto her bed. She wondered if what she was feeling was real happiness. She wasn't sure since it had been a long time since she had felt happy.

She rolled onto her stomach and laid her head on her hands. She could hardly believe that it had only been two days since the move. She felt as if this had been her home for years. Feeling safe and content, she rolled onto her back and fell back to sleep.

When she awoke a half-hour later, she pulled a clean dress from the cardboard box next to her bed. After carefully choosing a pair of shoes to match, she went downstairs.

When she reached the bottom of the stairs she stopped. She did not hear the familiar *drip, drip, ssssip* sound of her mother's coffee maker, or the shuffling sound her slippers made against the kitchen's black and white tile floor.

They're still asleep, she thought as she looked around. The house looked brighter and felt warmer than the day before. As she entered the parlor, she took note of how the sunlight flooded that room, causing its apricot colored walls to glow a soft peach color.

Standing in the middle of the largest room in the house, she could not help but feel lucky. Everything about the room was inviting. She closed her eyes and took a deep breath. She could almost smell the pine needles from the last Christmas tree that stood in the room. And . . . she could almost hear *Silent Night* being sung by family members as they gathered around a piano.

As she opened her eyes, she felt like she was living in a dream. She sat down on the sofa and scratched her head. "What happened to me last night to make me change my mind about the house?" she asked herself. "Something's happened to me and I can't explain it."

In need of answers, she thought back a couple of days, to the day her family moved to Dunville.

It was Penelope's first time inside the house. Standing in the foyer, she dropped her small, but heavy box to the floor with a loud *thud* that seemed to echo through the empty expanse of the house.

Mom's and Priscilla's heads snapped around.

"Oops! Sorry," Penelope said, embarrassed.

"It's okay. I guess that we're all feeling a little bit anxious right now. So . . . what do you guys think of the place?" Mom asked, turning first to Penelope.

"Uh . . . Um," she mumbled.

The expression on her mother's face let Penelope know how important it was for her family to like the house.

"Well, I need some time to look around first," she decided to say.

Mom smiled and gently patted her daughter's shoulder. "I'll be in the kitchen," she said as she disappeared through a door down the hall, alongside the main staircase.

Even though Penelope had seen no more of her new house than the town mail carrier had, she could not help but feel that her mother had made a big mistake. The damp, cold air that smelled like stale ice stung her nostrils and offered proof that this could never be *her* home. As she glanced around, a sour and sickeningly familiar feeling began to erupt in her stomach—it was the same feeling that she had the day her mother took her and Priscilla to see the house for the first time. She would never forget that day.

The weather was warm and sunny and a gentle breeze rustled the leaves of the huge old trees in the neighborhood. Penelope was excited because she was going to see her new home for the first time. Mom had said that it needed some work, but nothing prepared her for what she saw when they pulled into the driveway.

Looking up at the house with its enormous wise-eyed windows and strangely adorned, sagging roofline, she could not help but feel embarrassed to call the house *her* home.

"So, this is it?" she said, trying not to let her disappointment show.

"Yes . . . this is it," Mom replied proudly. "From the first time I saw this house, I knew that it was meant to be ours."

Penelope rolled up her window and got out of the car. A cold chill went down her spine as she followed the crumbling brick path to the house's front porch. The wrap-around porch, which probably had been painted white, but now looked gray and dingy, was peeling and warped. It was also covered with long ugly brown vines that looked like strange extensions of the bushes below. The house appeared to be trapped and held firm to the property like a prisoner.

This place is a nightmare, she thought. *It looks like a traditional haunted house. If it were night, a bat would probably fly past.*

Once they moved in, she would find that she was right. At night, the house looked as nightmarish as she had imagined. With its leaning silhouette, it took on an eerie appearance which seemed to beckon to the creatures of the night.

As Penelope climbed the porch steps, she smiled at her mother. She knew that she could not let her true feelings show.

"The realtor told me that this wonderful old Victorian was once the pride of the town. But, as you can see, it needs some work," Mom said as she motioned the girls to follow her. "The realtor also said that a married couple lived alone in this house for many years. They moved away about four years ago, and its been sitting vacant ever since."

Mom led the girls around the grounds as she continued to chatter on about the house. As Penelope followed her mother, her mind began to wander. She could not help but notice how both the house and its grounds were sick and dying from years of harsh weather and neglect. Looking at the house, she was almost sure that at one time it had been painted blue—like clear tropical water, but now the color was grayed. The shingles were chipped, and many of its original stained glass windows had been broken and replaced with ordinary glass. *It's such a shame*, she thought.

As Mom talked about her gardening plans, Priscilla noticed a small, dilapidated wooden shed leaning against the hedges on the North side of the yard. "Mom, what's that?" she asked, pointing to the structure.

"The realtor told me that the shed is very old. It may have been built before the house. I guess it was used to store gardening tools. Maybe we'll use it for that too."

Priscilla turned around to face the house. "I bet this house was really beautiful at one time, and I know that it will be again," she said, trying to sound positive.

Penelope's thoughts returned to her first time inside the house. *It's happening all over again*, she thought to herself as she stood in the foyer, staring at the massive oak staircase before her.

The finish on the wood, which must have glistened at one time, was now dull and scarred and some of the spindles leaned at strange angles. She wondered if it was safe.

"Come on girls—I want you to see something," Mom said, motioning for Penelope and her sister to follow. Penelope watched as her mother and sister hurried through an archway to the left of the foyer.

"I'll be right there," she called after them.

As she continued to look at the staircase, she began to think about her new bedroom somewhere on the second floor. *I hope my room has a fireplace*, she thought . . . *and it better have a big closet.*

Suddenly, her concerns about the safety of the staircase were no longer important. Without further hesitation, she grabbed the handrail, which felt as rough as tree bark, and placed her foot on the first step. "**Crash!**" Several of the rotted spindles broke away from the handrail and fell to the floor.

Priscilla bit her lip. "Great!"

Mom and Priscilla ran in from the other room. "Penelope, are you okay?" Mom asked, visibly concerned.

Assuring them that she was fine, Penelope decided that she could wait to see her bedroom and turned her attention to the parlor. Peeking through the archway, she was thrilled to find that the room had an enormous fireplace. She immediately ran over for a closer look.

"Mom, it's beautiful," she said as she ran her hand over its mantle, picking up an inch of chalky white dust.

"Look at the carvings," Mom suggested as she pointed to the small cherubs which ran along the base of the mantle.

Penelope gently ran her fingers over the smooth carved wood and smiled the biggest smile. "It's so beautiful."

"I haven't seen you smile like that in a long time."

"I guess you're right," Penelope said as she bent down and ran her fingers over the hearth. She was pleased to see that underneath the dust, the hearth appeared to be made of pink marble.

Standing up, she continued inspecting the room. Unfortunately, the water stains on the ceiling and the cracks in the walls dulled her enthusiasm once again. Walking around, she noticed the creaking sounds made by the dusty old floors and she felt a deep chill settle on her. *I just don't know about this place. It's in really bad shape,* she thought as she turned to her mother. But, remembering what she promised herself, she knew she had to lie.

"Mom, it's really great," she said with a smile.

Seemingly pleased with Penelope's response, Mom turned to Priscilla and asked her what she thought of the house. After a long pause, Priscilla answered, "Oh . . . yeah . . . it's great, Mom. All it needs is some cleaning up and a little TLC and it will feel like home."

"Well . . . good! I knew that you would both like it. Wait till you see the upstairs, and your rooms. Come on up you two," she said as she slowly climbed the rickety stairs, hugging the wall to avoid the handrail and grinning the whole way.

Sounds of footsteps and creaking stairs brought Penelope back to the present—to her third day living in her new house. It was Mom, and she was coming down the stairs. "What are you doing up so early?" she asked and yawned.

"Well, it's finally stopped raining, and I wanted to get a jump on the day," replied Penelope.

Mom raised an eyebrow. "I'm so glad to hear that," she said, shuffling into the kitchen. "What's caused the change in attitude?"

"I'm not sure," said Penelope.

"Maybe it was a good night's sleep," Mom suggested, smiling. "That always helps my mood."

"That could be it," Penelope said as she opened the refrigerator door.

Chapter Three

Priscilla Receives a Gift

*I*t was almost ten o'clock when Priscilla awoke. With the sands of sleep clinging steadfastly to her eyelids, she sat up slowly in bed. Feeling chilly, she gave her blue checked comforter a tug. "That's better," she said, pulling the comforter up under her chin.

Sleepily, she glanced around the room and rubbed her eyes. The walls were covered with stained and yellowed floral wallpaper, and a pair of matching, ruffled floral curtains hung on the room's single window. The room was much too feminine for Priscilla and, no doubt, had once belonged to a young girl. Priscilla had always dreamed of having a room of her own. Her room would be painted a rich shade of blue, and she would fill it with baseball memorabilia. Looking around the room once more, she decided that she would discuss her ideas with her mother later. *Maybe we can talk about it over a good breakfast,* she thought. *Hopefully Mom will go grocery shopping this morning.* The thought of eating another granola bar or bologna sandwich disgusted her.

All of a sudden, a delicious aroma tickled her nose—it was coming from the hallway. Was she dreaming or was it really home-cooked food—she had to find out. But before her feet touched the floor, there was a knock at the door and Mom poked her head in. "I'm glad to see that you're finally up," she said, smiling.

Priscilla sighed, "I had some really strange dreams last night."

"What were they about?"

"I'm not really sure, but I woke up in the middle of the night in a cold sweat."

"Are you feeling better this morning?" asked Mom, a look of mild concern in her eyes.

"Yeah . . . I guess so."

"Good! Now, come on downstairs. Your sister's been up since eight and has cooked us some breakfast," Mom said as she retreated, pulling the door closed behind her.

That's strange, Priscilla thought. *The Penelope I know never gets up early, and she certainly does not cook.*

While getting dressed, Priscilla could not stop thinking about her sister. "Why is she in such a good mood this morning, especially since she was so upset over what happened in town last night? I've got to see this for myself," she said as she hurried out of her room.

Entering the kitchen, she felt like she had just walked into a diner at breakfast time. The smell of bacon, eggs, coffee, flowers and cleaning solutions filled the air. She started to smile, but quickly remembered that she was annoyed with her sister.

"It's nice to see that you're alive," Penelope remarked as Priscilla came through the kitchen door.

Priscilla was not in the mood for another verbal catfight, so she ignored her sister and sat down at the table.

Mom, who had been cleaning the inside of the refrigerator, sat down too. "After breakfast, why don't you girls explore the rest of the house," she suggested, taking off her rubber gloves.

"That sounds okay to me," said Priscilla, glancing at her sister.

"Why don't we make a game out of it?" Penelope said, grinning.

Priscilla was shocked. "You're kidding, right? We haven't played anything together in a long time."

"Come on, let's go!" Penelope said as she shut off the stove. With a mischievous grin on her face, she removed her apron, threw it on a chair, and ran out of the kitchen.

"What about breakfast?" Priscilla called after her.

When Penelope did not answer, she grabbed a blueberry muffin off the counter and followed.

"Have fun you two," Mom called after her daughters.

Once they reached the foyer, Penelope insisted on leading the way. "Mom said the house has 13 rooms. Let's start on the second floor," she suggested and sprinted up the stairs.

Priscilla could not help but be suspicious of her sister's enthusiasm. "That sounds okay," she replied, raising her foot to the first step.

"Creeeeek, SNAP!" Priscilla felt her foot go through the step. When she looked down, she saw that the old wood of the step had crumbled like a stale cracker and now, her foot was stuck.

"Priscilla, what happened?" Penelope asked from atop the staircase.

"My foot went through the step and it's stuck!"

"I'll be right there," Penelope said with a hint of concern in her voice as she started back down the stairs.

"No! It's okay! I got it out."

"Good, now maybe we can get back to exploring the house," Penelope said as she once again headed back up the stairs.

Feeling a little weird, Priscilla sat down on the second step and called up to Penelope, "I'll be there in a minute."

"All right, I'll be in my bedroom . . . but don't take too long."

The sound of the stair splintering caused her to remember an unsettling incident that occurred on her first trip into town.

The rain had let up again, and Mom and Priscilla waited in the parlor for Penelope to come downstairs.

"I wish she would hurry up," Mom said glancing down at her watch. "It will be getting dark soon, and we'll have a harder time finding our way around."

Priscilla sat opposite her mother on the sofa, fumbling with her sneaker lace. She wished that she had enough guts to tell her mother how she really felt about going into town.

A few minutes later, Penelope announced that she was ready to go. Mom and Priscilla stood up and headed into the foyer. Penelope was standing at the top of the stairs, dressed in the yellow taffeta dress with matching shoes and purse that she wore to her Aunt Mary's wedding last year. Priscilla could not believe her sister's nerve. She wondered: *What is she trying to prove by dressing that way?*

Mom's face was the color of moldy cottage cheese and her eyes were as big as ping-pong balls.

"What's wrong with you two?" Penelope asked as she sauntered down the stairs and then over to the mirror.

"Penelope . . . we're only going into town to look around. Don't you think that's a little much?" Mom said in a soft voice.

"No, I don't! I want to make a good impression on our new neighbors," she replied, tossing her hair over her shoulder as she headed towards the door.

Mom and Priscilla exchanged disapproving looks and then followed.

Several blocks away, the streets of downtown Dunville glistened under the light cast by the colorful neon signs in the store windows. The setting sun also cast a light of its own over the sleepy town, transforming it into a living painting.

"Let's go into this store," Penelope suggested, pulling Mom in the direction of a small dress shop.

When they entered the shop, a bell that hung above the door tinkled pleasantly, like a miniature crystal wind chime swaying with a gentle breeze. The welcoming sound caused Priscilla to forget her suspicions for a moment. Once inside, she thought that the store had been decorated in "Early American Grandma". However, the wonderfully spicy floral aroma suggested that it was really a sophisticated boutique in disguise. To her right was a cozy beige sofa adorned with three ivory doilies. To her left, there was a rocking chair and a delicate antique desk. An oval coffee table was carefully placed in the store's center. *Yup, it's Grandma's house all right,* she thought.

"Can I help you?" asked a pretty woman with short brown hair and tiny blue eyes that sparkled like shiny beads.

"Hello—we're the Posts," Mom replied. "We just moved into the old house on Jackson Street. We decided to check out the stores in town, and since your shop looked so inviting, we decided to stop here first."

When Mom mentioned where they lived, the woman turned her eyes to the floor. "Are you all right?" Mom asked, when she noticed the woman was growing pale.

"Uh . . . yes. I forgot something in the storeroom. I'll be back in just a . . ." the woman's words trailed off as she backed away and disappeared behind a pink floral curtain.

Priscilla knew that the woman would not return. "Let's just go," she suggested.

Penelope, who had been searching through the racks of dresses that were surely overpriced, stopped and whined, "We can't go now. I haven't tried anything on yet."

Priscilla knew that arguing would do no good.

"Mom, would it be okay if I waited outside?" she asked, grasping the front door's brass handle.

Mom agreed, as long as she promised not to wander off. Outside, the wind had picked up, but Priscilla welcomed the fresh air. The strong spicy smell in the store was beginning to give her a headache. The sky was almost black and the streetlights had just come on, casting a pale green glow over the town. Priscilla felt protected from the rain and almost anything else while standing under the bright red awning of *Pat's Wear You Find It Dress Shop*.

All of a sudden she felt very tired. She sat down on the sidewalk and, as she rested her head against the rough brick of the shop, she heard the sound of twigs cracking under foot. The sound seemed to come from the narrow alley beside her. She wondered if someone was there, as she nervously peered into the alley. It was empty.

When she turned back around, she saw an eerie shadow blanketing the smooth cement in front of her. With butterflies in her stomach, she looked up and saw a tall heavy-set woman hovering over her and holding a crumpled, brown shopping bag. Slowly, Priscilla stood up. "It's you!" she said, timidly.

The woman did not speak, but Priscilla recognized her as the pipe-smoking woman who lived across the street from her. Up close, the woman had deep lines in her face and a strip of silvery brown hair above her lip. Although she did not say a word, Priscilla knew that the woman had come to see her. Maybe it was the look in her eyes—the same eyes that scared her a few hours earlier. Dark green and deeply set, she now saw a strange and different world there.

"I feel like we've already met," Priscilla stammered. "How did you know that I'd be here?"

The woman, who towered over Priscilla like a bear about to take her prey, grunted. Priscilla wasn't sure what to say next.

"Mmm . . . my name is Priscilla—what's your name?"

Without uttering a word, the woman raised her left hand and laid it on Priscilla's shoulder. The sheer weight of the woman's thick arm made her tremble.

"What do you want?" Priscilla asked, her voice shaking.

"Here, take this. Consider it a house warming gift," the woman grumbled as she handed Priscilla the shopping bag.

Priscilla reluctantly reached out her hand and accepted the bag. Opening it carefully, she saw a small bird wriggling at the bottom of the bag.

"Why did you give me a . . ." she started to ask, glancing up.

The woman had disappeared.

Once again, Priscilla peered into the narrow alley and decided that the woman did not go that way.

"Let's get you out of this bag," she said, gently picking up the bird.

In the soft light that filtered through the shop's large window, she could see the bird's color clearly. "You're so beautiful," she whispered. "I've never seen a bird that was the color of a summer sky before."

The bird looked up at Priscilla with tiny eyes resembling black raindrops, but it did not move.

"What's wrong with you? Can't you fly?"

As if responding to her question, the tiny bird tried to flutter its wings.

Priscilla noticed a gaping wound about the size of a raisin under the bird's right wing. "What happened to you little bird? Did that strange woman do this to you?"

As before, the bird didn't move, but only peered up at Priscilla with its mournful eyes.

"That's okay . . . you don't have to try to move. I'll take care of you," she said, cradling the bird in her arms.

Moments later, Mom and Penelope came out of the store. Penelope was in tears. "I don't understand it—the dressing room was locked, and the woman didn't come back," she cried.

"Come on Priscilla—let's all go home!" Mom said, taking Penelope by the arm.

"Wait!" Priscilla protested. "I have something to show you."

She held up the frightened bird and Mom took a step back. "Where did you get *that?*" she asked.

Priscilla explained how their new neighbor from across the street gave it to her. "I don't know why she gave it to me, but I want to take care of it," she said.

Suddenly, Priscilla's thoughts about the bird were gone—driven away by Penelope's shrill voice.

"**Come on! What are you doing down there?**" Penelope shrieked from the top of the stairs. "I've been in my room waiting for you for over 15 minutes."

Normally, Priscilla would have shrieked back, but this time she didn't.

"I'm coming. I was just thinking," she said as she sprinted up the stairs.

The second floor of the house, with its maze-like hallways and secret passageways, was a mystical place. It allowed Penelope and Priscilla's imaginations to run free. It also let their adventurous sides take over.

"This house is amazing! It's like an enormous and mysterious old playground," Priscilla said as she turned a corner and saw a door that was smaller than the others.

"Hey, Penelope, look at this door! It's so little," Priscilla said as she pointed to the door, which appeared to be about four feet tall.

Before Penelope could answer, Priscilla asked, "Where do you think such a small door could lead?" Her hand was already on the doorknob.

"Maybe it is a secret door that no one is supposed to know about. And . . . maybe it leads to the attic . . . the place where the boogie man lives!" replied Penelope, wiggling her fingers above her sister's head.

"Hey! You're not scaring me. I know for a fact that the attic door is next to Mom's room. This door probably opens to another closet . . . a child's closet, or something," Priscilla said as she quickly opened the door.

"**Aarrhhh!**"

Both girls screamed as a fat brown rat ran out from the closet.

"*Screeech, screeech*," it squealed as it ran between their legs.

Penelope jumped. **"Aarrhhh! I think it touched me."**

She was right. The rat's tail brushed against her ankle as it scurried by. Together, ever so slowly, the girls turned around to see where the rat had gone. Halfway down the hall, it stopped, turned around, and looked back at the girls. Priscilla felt as if the rat with its tiny, black beady eyes was trying to tell her something.

"He'll be back," she muttered to herself.

A moment later, all that she could see was the tip of a long skinny tail disappearing into a small opening near the back stairs.

"Boy, he was huge. I didn't know that rats could get that big," Priscilla added.

"I know . . . what do you think he's been eating?"

"I don't want to think about that! Let's go tell Mom what happened."

When Mom heard there was a rat in the house, she immediately called the town exterminator, *Rid-O-Pests*. Priscilla could hear the frustration in her mother's voice when she had to repeat her address several times. After a long pause, she slammed down the phone.

"You are *not* going to believe this," she said. "The woman from the exterminating company just hung up on me. What's wrong with the people in this town? First the woman from the dress shop, and now this. It's a good thing I found work outside of town or we'd be in big trouble."

"I was right—it is the whole town," Priscilla said aloud. When she realized what she had just said, she was embarrassed.

"What do you mean by that?" Penelope asked.

Priscilla could feel something sour erupting in the pit of her stomach. "Uh, I just meant that the town needs time to . . . to get to know us."

Suddenly, the corners of Mom's mouth turned up and, for a moment, she looked like the Cheshire Cat in *Alice in Wonderland.* "Priscilla has given me a great idea. I think our new neighbors are probably just nervous about outsiders. We should really make the effort to get to know them."

"Maybe we should have a party and invite everyone in the neighborhood," Penelope added.

Priscilla could not believe her ears. She wondered: *Do they actually think that a party is the answer?*

"Priscilla, what do you think about that idea?" Mom asked.

Priscilla cracked a smile. "I think that Penelope will organize a great party."

Later that night as she lay in bed, Priscilla wondered if she had really seen glimpses of the old Penelope or was she imagining it. *I think that we grew a tiny bit closer today,* she thought, holding Ashford tightly.

On the verge of sleep, she heard the wind. It sounded furious as it whistled through the old maple tree outside her window, rustling its leaves. The wounded bird, which she named Tikki, was also restless. She could hear the young bird fluttering its good wing against the dulled metal bars of his new home, the old hamster cage that she had placed near the radiator.

"It's okay little guy," she said in a gentle voice. "It's only the wind."

Her voice seemed to sooth the bird and, in turn, the bird chirped a soft lullaby. When the bird became quiet, so did the wind. All was quiet for the first time since she slipped into bed. Her body began to welcome the darkness and stillness of her room. Like a dream, out of the walls of her room came a voice like a familiar friend. "I will help you."

Chapter Four

Penelope Encounters a Wild Beast

With the memories of her disastrous shopping trip long forgotten, Penelope concerned herself with more important issues. Sauntering back and forth in her favorite red high heel sandals, she checked out her room.

I have to say—Mom was right about the white eyelet curtains. They go perfectly with the white lace throw pillows. Next, she slipped off her shoes and walked over to where a picture of her favorite rock group, *The No Names*, hung crookedly on the wall. After straightening the picture, she smiled. She was pleased with her choice of sunflower yellow paint and with how much she had accomplished in only a week. The room had definitely exceeded her vision of the perfect bedroom.

Even though her room was wonderful and the house had won a place in her heart, something was missing. She plopped down on her bed and grabbed one of her new pink silk throw pillows. She began to think about her relationship with her sister. Judging from Priscilla's recent behavior, Penelope felt she couldn't count on her. *All we do is fight, she just doesn't seem to understand me anymore*, she thought.

Suddenly, she smiled. *What I really need to do is make some new friends.* Back in the city, she had lots of friends and figured that the housewarming party would be a great way to introduce herself to the community.

After lunch, she grabbed a pad of paper, a pen, her favorite purple beach towel, and a couple of her favorite fashion magazines and went out to the backyard.

It was a gorgeous sunny day, although slightly cool for mid-August. She spotted a rusty old aluminum lawn chair leaning against the house and dragged it over near the dying, brown hedges that lined the yard. Smiling to herself, she draped the towel over the chair, plopped down into it, and began flipping through her magazines.

No one knows me in this town. I can be anyone I want to be, she thought. *That's just what I'm going to do—re-invent myself, starting with a makeover.* And, she would do it in time for the party.

As she continued to flip through her magazine, she wiggled her toes in the dry blades of grass. Suddenly, she heard a strange crunching sound coming from the hedges behind her. She smiled as she pictured a mouse dancing on a bag of potato chips. Curious, she leaned over to inspect the hedge.

Peering into the mass of dry branches and seeing nothing out of the ordinary, she let out a sigh of relief.

"There's nothing there," she said to herself as she sat back in her chair.

When she returned to her magazine, she heard the noise again. This time, she did not have time to inspect. Something jumped out of the hedges and landed in her lap. **"Aarrhhh! Aarrhhh! Aarrhhh!** She screamed so loud that the creature bounced off her lap, onto the ground, and scurried away. **"GET IT OFF ME! GET IT OFF ME!"**

Responding to Penelope's cries, Mom ran out into the yard. **"What's wrong?"**

Tears were streaming down Penelope's face. "I was just sitting here reading . . . when some kind of wild beast jumped out of the hedges and attacked me."

As Mom comforted Penelope, Priscilla came running out of the house visibly concerned. **"What's going on out here?"**

"Some kind of animal attacked your sister."

"Was it another rat?"

"No! It was some kind of monster with orange hair, big sharp teeth, and long pointy claws," Penelope cried.

"That sounds like the cat from across the street," said Priscilla.

"A *cat?*" asked Penelope looking embarrassed. "But, it was so savage. It *couldn't* be a cat!"

"Maybe Priscilla's right, honey? I saw a big orange cat nosing around in our garden a couple of times," Mom said as she put her arms around Penelope. "Come on into the house and I'll get you a tissue and something to drink."

The next day, Penelope and Priscilla sat on the floor in Penelope's favorite room: the fireplace room.

The fireplace room was the second largest room in the house and, like Penelope's room; it also had a wonderful view of the neighbor's rose garden.

The light that entered the room through a pair of long narrow windows imparted a warm glow that softened the grassy-green color of the walls. She hoped that this light would also help to warm the bare oak floors that stretched endlessly throughout the house when winter came.

"I feel so silly for freaking out like that yesterday," Penelope said. "I don't know why I got so scared." Rolling over onto her stomach and looking around the room, she thought about everything that had happened since they moved into the house. "All in all, I feel pretty safe here. There's something about this house that makes me feel like everything is going to be all right. Do you get that feeling too?" she whispered.

Priscilla did not answer right away.

"You know what . . . I think I do. There's something different about this house. Nothing interesting ever happened in our old house."

"Do you realize that we have seen every part of this house, except for the attic?" Penelope asked.

"Yeah . . . and that's because it's dark and creepy. And besides, Mom said that we shouldn't go up there."

"Why not? I thought that you liked a little adventure. Are you scared?"

Priscilla thought about it for a moment. "I do like adventure, but it's too dark up there. We won't be able to see anything."

The girls were quiet for a moment before Penelope said, "Well . . . maybe we can find a flashlight."

After a long pause, Priscilla said, "Okay, let's go!"

Chapter Five

Follow the Light Priscilla

*A*fter grabbing a flashlight from the pantry, the girls headed upstairs and down the long hallway. When they reached the attic door, Priscilla noticed that the air smelled stale. She bent down and realized that the odor was wafting in from under the door.

"Penelope, it smells like your socks," she said, making a face.

Penelope made a face back. "Ha, ha—very funny. What are you waiting for? Open the door!" she said, nudging her sister.

"Don't rush me!" Priscilla snapped, and turned the doorknob.

"Stop! Wait!" said Penelope. "Don't open it! There's a light coming from under the door."

Priscilla removed her hand from the doorknob. All of a sudden, what had been a soft glow became as bright as a roaring fire. The girls backed away from the door and Penelope grabbed tightly onto her sister's arm.

"Why are you grabbing onto me? I'm as afraid as you are!"

"I guess I'm not as ready for this as I thought."

"It's okay, we'll protect each other," Priscilla said, trying to be comforting. "Now, stand back."

"Okay, but be careful."

For a second, Priscilla stood frozen. She could hardly believe that those words came out of her mouth. It was as if a voice deep within her said, "It's up to you this time."

"Don't be afraid," she told herself before lifting her left arm to shield her head. She had no idea what she would find on the other side of the door. Gaining confidence that she didn't know she had, she slowly turned the doorknob and pulled the door open.

A blast of hot and extremely musty air shot out from the attic stairway, knocking the girls back against the wall.

"Wow! That was intense!" Priscilla said as she tried to stand up.

Penelope, who looked like she was pretty shaken, did not say a word.

"I guess the attic has been closed for a long time," Priscilla added as she helped Penelope to her feet.

Cautiously, Penelope peered through the doorway. "That's strange, I can still feel the heat," she said, carefully taking a step forward. "What happened to the light? There's no light of any kind up there now. This is definitely the creepiest place in the whole house. I think I've changed my mind. I'm *not* going up there."

Penelope moved away from the stairs and handed the flashlight to her sister. "It's all yours. Let me know what you find up there. I'm going downstairs to get a snack."

"**Now who's the scaredy cat?**" Priscilla shouted to her sister, who disappeared down the hallway.

Peering up into the darkness, Priscilla wasn't going to take another step until she turned on the flashlight. In the narrow ribbon of light, she saw that in addition to being dark and creepy, the stairway was also narrow and curved. As she stood there unable to move, something deep within her urged her to continue. She did not fight the feeling, but rather welcomed it.

Step by step, she slowly crept up the stairs with the narrow beam from her flashlight lighting the way. Coming around the curve, she was surprised to see the soft glow of a small light coming from above. *Where is that light coming from? Mom told us there were no lights in the attic.*

Almost to the top, the flashlight went dead.

"It's just my luck," Priscilla grumbled and shoved the flashlight into the back pocket of her shorts.

The musty smell that seemed to follow the soft rays of light intensified as she neared the top. Keeping her eye on the light, she quickened her pace and soon reached the attic floor. Just as she began searching for the source of the mysterious light, it disappeared. She scanned the darkness of the attic room, but saw nothing. Then, out of nowhere, the light appeared again.

"There it is!"

The soft silvery light was glowing and pulsating in the distance, but it did not dispel the darkness of the room. Feeling her way past some boxes, and what felt like a bicycle, she could almost see the source of the light.

"**Ouch!**" She had bumped her knee on something pointy, and, as she rubbed it, she lost her balance and knocked into a pile of boxes.

"**Crash!**" The boxes fell to the floor.

When she lifted her head, she could clearly see that the light, which from a distance had appeared to glow softly, now flooded the room, shooting upward from a round wooden box on the floor. She immediately thought of a hot air balloon and of the burst of flame that shot up, heating the air inside the balloon, causing it to ascend. The box, which was about the size of her grandmother's apple pie, was tightly wedged between two broken wicker chairs and a tired looking sofa. The chairs and sofa surrounded the box like protective walls.

Moving closer, she cupped her hands above her eyes to protect them from the harsh rays. She now could see that the light was actually flowing from under a loosely fitted box lid. Priscilla wondered: *How bright would this light be if there was no lid?* All of a sudden, the light turned golden.

"This must be a dream," she said to herself, moving still closer. The light glowed with the intensity of a million fireflies. *I can't believe what I'm seeing,* she thought as she shielded her face with her forearm.

As she stood in awe of this truly magical sight, she felt for the first time that something wonderful and mystical dwelled within her house, and she felt very lucky to be a part of it.

With a new found courage, she bent down to remove the lid. But, when her hand pierced the light, she was thrown to the floor.

"Who would have thought that something so beautiful could be so dangerous," she said to herself as she tried to stand up.

She wondered how she could remove the lid without hitting the light again. As if someone had read her mind, the light faded once again to a soft glow. From behind her, a voice whispered, "Hurry! Open it! There's not much time!"

Priscilla turned around slowly, but no one was there. She was not afraid, but instead felt more strongly about her mission. As she lifted the lid, darkness filled the room once again. The light had disappeared as mysteriously and as quickly as it had appeared on the stairway.

"What happened? I can't see a thing," she cried.

Again, there was a whisper. It seemed to be all around her. "Don't be afraid—I'll help you."

"Who are you?" Priscilla called out as she strained to see through the blackness that surrounded her.

When no one answered she became frightened for the first time since she entered the attic. All she could do now was try to find her way back to the stairway, but not without the box. She knelt down on the dusty floor, felt around till she found her treasure, and then, after locating the lid, placed it firmly on the box. Holding it close to her body, she turned towards the stairs. As she took a step forward, she saw a dim light out of the corner of her eye. When she turned around, she noticed something that wasn't there before. It was a small window in the furthest corner of the attic. The round window let in just enough light to help her find her way back to the staircase. Fearful of losing the light, she hurried towards the stairs.

On the stairs, she had to once again deal with darkness. But, this time it was different. She felt stronger and more confident than before.

When Priscilla opened the attic door onto the second floor hallway, she found Penelope sitting on the floor with her arms crossed in front of her. "What happened up there? What did you see? You were up there for a long time."

"You should have come with me . . . but maybe its better that you didn't," Priscilla replied as she joined her sister on the floor. "It was touch and go for a minute or two."

"What do you mean by that?"

"Oh, nothing . . . my journey into the attic was just an amazing experience," Priscilla exclaimed, producing the box she had been hiding behind her back.

"What's that?" Penelope asked, her eyes sparkling.

"I found it upstairs. A magical glowing light led me to it. I have no idea what's inside."

Penelope gave her sister a strange look. "Yeah, right!" she said making a face. "Why don't you just open it?"

"No, why don't you open it," Priscilla said with a mischievous grin, and pushed the box towards her sister.

"Okay, I will," Penelope said confidently.

In the box, under what looked like blue straw, was a doll. "What a strange looking doll," Penelope cried. "No wonder someone left it up there."

"I don't think it's strange looking. I think it's pretty cool," Priscilla said, gently picking up the doll.

"It looks old and I think it's handmade. I wonder what it's supposed to be," Priscilla said as she ran her fingers over its painted face, which seemed to be made of wood. "Look Penelope, he's even wearing a tiny gold earring."

The doll was only slightly larger than Priscilla's hand and looked like a little old man with long black hair streaked with silver. He was wearing thin white pants that were tied with a small piece of gold string, a brown shirt, and a long white robe trimmed in gold. On his feet, he wore black sandals made from tiny strips of black leather.

The doll was also wearing a headband covered with sparkling red, blue and green jewels. "Those jewels are really cool. I wonder if they're real."

"I doubt it," snapped Penelope. "I think they're tacky."

"This is the strangest looking doll that I have ever seen," Penelope said as she grabbed the doll away from her sister. "Look at his smile. He looks like he's hiding something. What kind of girl would play with a dishonest doll?"

"I don't think he looks dishonest and besides, maybe he belonged to a boy," Priscilla replied as she grabbed the doll back.

Penelope shrugged.

"Boy or girl, I think he's great—I'm going to keep him," said Priscilla.

Later that day, the girls met in the fireplace room and started to write out invitations for the house-warming party. When Priscilla finished her pile, she decided it was time she told her sister what really happened in the attic.

"Penelope, please listen to me. I know that you don't believe in magic, but you have to believe me when I tell you that something incredible happened to me. Ever since I went up into the attic, I feel different."

Penelope was curled up on the window seat holding a pad and pen. "Different in what way?"

"I feel stronger and more self-confident than I have in my whole life. I think that I feel this way because of what happened to me in the attic. I also think that the house is trying to communicate with me."

Penelope started to giggle. "Are you joking? Houses can't talk or make things happen."

"I know that it sounds crazy, but I've been hearing things . . . and then, after what happened in the attic . . . I don't know . . . maybe I've finally lost it for good."

"Calm down Priscilla! I agree that this house has had a strange affect on all of us, but I doubt that it has anything to do with magic. Magic can only lead to no good."

Priscilla noticed that her sister's expression had changed the moment she said the word *magic.*

"Are you okay, Penelope? What did you mean by what you just said?"

Penelope opened her mouth as if to say something but stopped. Instead, she glanced down at her paper and began writing. "Now, if you're done talking crazy, maybe we can get back to writing out these invitations. Remember, we only have two days until the party," she said, finally.

No matter what her sister said, Priscilla was not going to forget about what happened in the attic or her suspicions. After the party, she planned to find out more about the house.

"You're right. Let's get back to business," she agreed and picked up an invitation.

Later that evening, Priscilla slipped outside and put an invitation into each and every one of the 35 mailboxes on the street. On her way back to her house, she noticed that the strange woman across the street was sitting on her porch, smoking her pipe. Like before, Priscilla felt the woman's eyes on her. *Why is she always staring at me? And our house—she stares at our house, too. What is she looking to find?*

Before parking her bike in the garage, Priscilla glanced back over her shoulder. The woman was no longer there."

Chapter Six

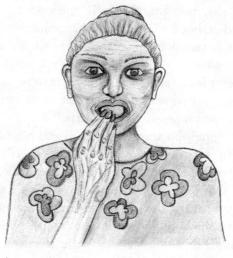

Penelope Takes a Stand

It was Friday morning, the day of the big party. Penelope was so excited about meeting her new neighbors that she got up extra early.

"We have balloons, crepe paper, party lights, and hats," she said to herself as she sat at the kitchen table with her list.

The sun was rising, but the kitchen still felt cool. Penelope was practically glowing as she thought about all of the new friends she was going to make. But before that could happen, there was much to do. Everything had to be perfect.

Mom shuffled into the kitchen and grabbed a cup out of the cabinet. "Good morning, sunshine," she said, smiling.

"Good morning, Mom," Penelope replied as she stood up and grabbed a bowl from the cabinet.

Mom started to fill the coffeepot with water. "So, today's our big day."

"Yes it is . . . and I want the party to be perfect."

Mom sat down at the table next to Penelope. "Don't worry so much—it's just a party."

Penelope's lip started to twitch and her face turned a soft shade of fuchsia. "Are you kidding? It's not just a party—it's an opportunity to meet our neighbors—the opportunity that I've been waiting for since we moved here." On the verge of tears, she put down her spoon and stood up. "I wish that somebody would think about my feelings for a change!" With a tear in her eye, she stormed out of the room.

Later that day, Penelope apologized to her mother for her outburst. She realized that Mom could not have known how important the party was to her. After making up, they worked side-by-side to finish decorating the parlor. They also discussed the menu and how many people they expected would attend.

"Well, Priscilla delivered 35 invitations; so, I would hope that at least half would be able to come," said Mom.

Penelope scrunched up her face and the corners of her mouth turned down like two wilting flowers. "Well— that's not good enough. I'm expecting everyone to come," she replied as she handed Mom a bunch of daisies from the nearby refreshment table.

Mom accepted the flowers in silence and did not say another word until after the decorating was complete.

The two stood in the parlor admiring their work.

"It's beautiful!" Penelope said, running her fingers over one of the white lace tablecloths.

Tiny pink and green lights were carefully strung around the windows, and small crystal vases filled with assorted garden flowers adorned the room's tables and window ledges. Colorful paper lanterns hung from the ceiling and pearly white balloons bobbed around on the floor.

"I can't wait to see the expressions on each neighbor's face when they are greeted at the door with the sweet smell of honeysuckle and roses," she added, taking in the precious aroma.

Mom only nodded. She appeared lost in thought.

"Mom—what's wrong?" Penelope asked as she smelled one of the roses.

Mom turned her attention to her daughter. "I was just thinking about Grandma. I wish she were able to be here. She, too, was looking forward to meeting some of our new neighbors."

"I wish she could be here too but, if she's sick, it's definitely better if she stays in bed," Penelope replied as she glanced at the mantel clock. She started to panic.

"Mom, I have to go and get ready. When I'm done, I'll help you finish in here," she said as she ran out of the room.

Upstairs in her room, she worked quickly to throw her new look together.

"Just a little more eye shadow and I'm ready," she said to herself as she opened her dresser drawer.

Since Penelope was a little girl, she liked to wear make-up—more specifically, her mother's make-up. With Priscilla standing watch, Penelope would sneak into her mother's bedroom, grab a tube of lipstick and whatever else caught her eye, and run back to her room as fast as she could.

Looking at the clock on her nightstand, she saw that it was almost time for the guests to arrive.

Shoot . . . I was supposed to help Mom in the kitchen, she remembered, *but once she sees why I wasn't there, she won't be upset. Oh, well!* she thought as she darted from her room.

From the top of the stairs, she could hear Mom and Priscilla in the parlor. Slowly and gracefully, she made her way down the stairs. When she reached the bottom, she called, "I'm ready! Come and see the new Penelope!"

Mom and Priscilla came rushing into the foyer. "Penelope—is that you?" Mom asked, looking surprised.

"Ha, ha—very funny. Of course it's me," Penelope replied as she sauntered past them and into the parlor.

Mom and Priscilla followed her.

Penelope was wearing a short, tight, black fuzzy-looking dress and black knee-high boots that made her feel mature and sophisticated. Her pretty face was covered with gobs of rose-colored blush. She had smothered her lips with bright red lipstick, and thickly coated her eyelashes with black mascara and her eyelids with green eye shadow. For a crowning touch, her long blond hair was neatly piled on top of her head in a tight bun, fastened with about a dozen sparkling hairpins.

Before sitting down on the sofa, she smoothed her dress one last time. "Really Mom—what do you think of my new look?" she asked, smiling.

Mom's eyes widened. "You look very mature," she replied, tilting her head. "Is that my make-up you're wearing?"

Penelope sighed a breath of relief when her sister interrupted.

"What happened to you?" That hair . . . that dress, and all of that eye shadow! And, by the way, *where* did you get those clothes?"

Penelope turned her attention back to her mother, who also appeared to be waiting for an answer. Later she would tell them that after buying the party supplies, her grandmother took her to the mall. But right now, she could not afford to get herself worked up.

"Mom, I hope you don't mind that I borrowed a few things."

"Actually Penelope, I do mind. You know how I feel about your wearing make-up. We've talked about this about a dozen times before," Mom said as she sat down next to her daughter. "Why do you have this sudden need to look older?"

At that moment Penelope felt very alone. Tears welled up in her eyes. "What is this—an interrogation?" she asked, beginning to sob. "But, if you must know, I thought that a change would be good for me."

Mom put her arm around Penelope. "I'm sorry honey. I didn't mean to hurt your feelings, but I think you are beautiful just the way you are."

"I guess you're entitled to your opinion."

"We'll talk about this later," Mom said.

Everyone sat in silence until the doorbell rang at 15 minutes past six. "**Buzzzzz!**"

Penelope jumped.

Priscilla and Mom looked at each other, but did not speak.

"Whoever it is . . . they're late," Penelope said angrily as she ran to the door.

Mom and Priscilla followed.

When Penelope opened the door, a tall hefty woman with skin like crumpled tissue paper pushed past her. She wore her hair in a tight bun, which caused her thin gray eyebrows to be pulled up so high that they almost met with her hairline. As Penelope stared at the neighbor who lived across the street, she thought that she had looked much creepier from a distance. Even her dark eyes appeared warmer and friendlier.

Like a cowboy trying to lasso a steer, Mom hooked the woman's massive arm as she walked by. "Please let me show you to the parlor. My name is Frances Post. These are my daughters, Penelope and Priscilla," she said with a warm smile.

The woman, who wore a turquoise blue and green floral dress, a pilled grass green sweater, and scuffed white dress shoes, continued through the archway leading into the parlor. Mom, Penelope, and Priscilla followed closely behind. Penelope noticed that the woman walked with a limp and had a large hole in her pantyhose, just above her thick ankle.

"Please make yourself comfortable. Can I get you something to eat or drink?" Mom asked, showing the woman to the sofa.

The woman did not sit, but turned around and headed straight towards the refreshment table. As she passed by, Penelope noticed she smelled of alcohol and fish. Within seconds, the strange woman was inhaling the hors d'oeuvres, two at a time. Priscilla crept over to Penelope's side.

"She lives across the street from us in that white colonial."

"I know. I've seen her."

"She smokes a pipe and sits on her porch staring at our house. She's the one who gave me Tikki."

Penelope sighed heavily and rolled her eyes. "Are you finished? So she stares and gives people wounded birds—you don't really know anything about her. And besides, she can't be that bad—she came to our party, didn't she?"

Priscilla paused for a moment. "Maybe you're right, but she still gives me the creeps."

"Don't be so rude . . . we should at least see what she has to say."

Priscilla shrugged her shoulders and together the girls made their way over to where Mom was talking to their guest.

"So . . . I'm sorry, I didn't get your name?" Mom inquired, offering the woman a seat.

The woman paid no attention to the question—she was too busy shoving puffed cheese balls and little roasted sausages into her mouth. Mom waited a few minutes and then asked the question again. This time the woman mumbled, "Mrs. Maven," without looking up from the table.

"Well, it's nice to meet you Mrs. Maven," Mom replied.

Penelope, who was sitting on the sofa, watched in disgust as the woman finished off the platter of fish nuggets and tartar sauce.

Every attempt was made to strike up a normal conversation with Mrs. Maven, but every attempt failed. Nothing seemed to matter but the food.

"Pssst! Mom! It's almost seven thirty. Do you think that anyone else is coming?" Priscilla whispered.

"I'm sure that more people will be here, they're just running late."

Penelope turned around on the sofa and looked out the picture window. She saw that the street was empty. *It's hopeless*, she thought to herself as she choked back the tears. *No one else is coming.*

After Mrs. Maven finished eating, she began to walk around the room, her shoes squeaking with every step she took.

"What is she doing?" Penelope asked. "If she isn't going to talk to us, why doesn't she just leave? This party is a disaster!"

Another half-hour went by and Mrs. Maven was nowhere to be found. Mom came up behind Penelope and put her hands on her shoulders. "Honey—I'm so sorry that this night didn't turn out the way you had hoped. I know how much it meant to you," she said and yawned.

"It's okay," Penelope mumbled.

"If it's okay with you, I'm going to start cleaning up. Will one of you please go and find Mrs. Maven and tell her that it's time to leave."

The girls looked at each other.

"I'll go," offered Penelope, looking at her sister. "You should stay here and help Mom."

Priscilla agreed and began to clear away the empty platters.

Upstairs, Penelope found Mrs. Maven in Priscilla's room, crouched down next to Tikki's cage.

"**Hey—what are you doing there?**" Penelope shouted. "This is my sister's room. You don't belong in here. The party is over, so please leave."

Without saying a word, Mrs. Maven waddled back downstairs and walked out the front door. Behind her, the smell of alcohol and fish lingered in the air.

Mom and Priscilla had been hurrying back and forth between the parlor and the kitchen, collecting unused glasses and plates, putting them in the cabinets, and then heading back for more.

"This was the strangest party I've ever been to," Priscilla said as she looked around the room.

"I can't understand it either . . . and that woman . . . she was so rude," added Mom.

"And nosy, too," said Penelope as she stood in the archway and removed her hairpins, one-by-one.

"What do you mean?" asked Priscilla

Penelope explained how she found Mrs. Maven in Priscilla's room talking to her bird.

"You're kidding! Is Tikki okay? I hope she didn't take anything," Priscilla said anxiously as Mom handed her another clean glass.

Penelope shuffled into the parlor, plopped down on the sofa, and shook out her hair. "I don't think so, but she seemed to be pretty interested in Tikki, though."

"I'll go up and check my room when we're through here, "Priscilla said as she headed to the kitchen.

As Penelope helped clean up, her disappointment quickly turned to anger. She decided that she needed to confront the people who ignored her invitation.

"I plan to find out why we're not good enough for the people of this town . . . and I'm going to do it first thing in the morning," she said to herself.

Penelope got up early the following morning in order to confront her neighbors before they went to work. Sleep did not dull her fury or desire for answers.

"Ignore my invitation, will you . . . I will not tolerate that!" she said angrily as she slipped out of bed and headed to her closet. "We've put up with enough from you people!"

For the first time since she moved to Dunville, Penelope's eyes were open. She realized that her sister was right—there was something *very* wrong with the townspeople.

"When I show up on their doorsteps, they will have to talk to me," she said to herself as she dressed.

With fire in her eyes, she left the house. "Ignore me, did they! Well, they obviously don't know who I am!" she ranted, squinting her eyes and wrinkling her nose.

Outside, the neighborhood was quiet, except for a pair of squirrels playing in the trees overhead. One-by-one, she went up to the house of each and every neighbor who was invited to her party, she rang the doorbell, and she knocked on the door. And one-by-one, no one answered.

About halfway down Jackson Street, she stood in front of an incredibly beautiful rose-colored Victorian house. She rushed up to the front door and rang the bell. As she was about to knock, a girl about her age answered the door. "Hello. Can I help you?"

The girl was as thin as a flagpole and almost as tall. She had short brown hair that she wore tucked behind her ears and her eyes were the color of coffee beans. Penelope smiled when she saw how the girl was dressed. She was wearing a short black suede skirt, red knee socks, and a short red tank top that exposed her stomach. *Wow!* She thought.

This was the look that she desired—sleek and put together. Looking down at the girl's shoes, she smiled even brighter. She had to know where the girl shopped, but didn't dare ask. Black, chunky, and covered in silver studs, she thought that the girl's shoes made the outfit work.

"Hi . . . my name is Penelope Post," she said finally.

The girl did not reply, but she continued to gnaw on her bubble gum.

"I . . . I . . . invited your family to . . . a party at our house," Penelope stammered.

"When is it?"

"Well, it was last night."

"Oh. Well, I didn't know anything about it. So, how was it anyway?"

"Terrible! No one showed up except for a strange old lady who lives across the street from us."

"Where do you live?"

The question surprised Penelope because she thought that everyone in town had heard about them.

"I live down the street, number *301*," she said nervously.

"Okay. Well, thanks for stopping by," the girl quickly replied, and began to shut the door.

"I like your shoes," Penelope blurted out.

The girl stopped and looked at her. "Thanks. I like yours too. By the way, my name is Jasmine."

As Penelope stood in the doorway talking to the girl, she felt that there was something familiar and comfortable about her, and that she could easily be friends with her. It was probably her keen sense of style . . . or, was it something else?

On her way home, she figured it out. She and Jasmine were alike—it was as simple as that. Walking up to her house, Penelope looked across the street and noticed Mrs. Maven sitting on her porch, staring at her.

"Hello, Mrs. Maven!"

Mrs. Maven did not return the greeting, but leaned over the porch and called out, "Pumpkin—come here, Pumpkin."

A moment later, a ratty orange-striped cat wearing a red collar came running up the steps and jumped into Mrs. Maven's lap.

Seeing the cat, Penelope gasped. "That's the beast that tried to attack me," she said to herself.

Feeling slightly spooked, she hurried up her porch steps and into the house.

Chapter Seven

Priscilla Searches for Answers

*I*t was Monday morning and Priscilla was glad that the party was behind her. It was time for her to find out more about her house. Standing in front of her bedroom window, she wondered about the new girl in her sister's life. Part of her was glad that her sister made a new friend, and part of her was afraid she was losing her sister. *I hope they don't become too close,* she thought as she sat down on a bench next to the window and put on her sneakers.

Now ready to go, she wanted to see if her mother's car was still in the drive, so she headed down to the front bedroom to look out the window. It was seven forty-five and her mother should have left for work already.

"Darn, Mom's still here!"

While she waited for her to leave, she sat down on the room's only piece of furniture, a tattered old brown corduroy recliner, and went over her plan.

"Once Mom leaves, I'll sneak out and head over to the library. They open at ten, and I'll be there at exactly that time. After I get the information I need, I'll hurry back here and Penelope will never know I've left."

At a quarter past eight, Priscilla heard the *screeeech-brrrooom* of her mother's car, and flew down the stairs like a dog on a chase. When she reached the parlor window, she watched as her mother's car sped away.

"Finally—she's gone!"

After waiting five minutes just to make sure her mother would not be back, she slipped out the front door. Outside, she watched a short slender man with thick, fake-looking, salt and pepper-colored hair get in his car and drive away. Afraid of being seen by anyone, she ducked behind an evergreen tree before dashing across Jackson Street. When she reached Third Avenue, the wind whipped up suddenly and she quickened her pace as if afraid of being swept away.

"This is crazy! Why am I hurrying?" she asked herself as she neared Lincoln Avenue. The library was just a little further up the road.

When she reached Lincoln Avenue, she no longer heard or felt the wind—it was as if it was holding its breath. Priscilla didn't know how, but she knew the stillness would not last. She also knew that something was coming— something more savage than the wind. And, she was right! A moment later, she started to hear what sounded like voices furiously whirling around her and whipping her braids into her face. She was beginning to feel dizzy.

"*Something should be done about that house! It's an eyesore! It should be torn down!*" the voices taunted.

Frightened, Priscilla tried to run, but she was having trouble standing.

"LEAVE ME ALONE!" she screamed and looked around for help. Not seeing anyone, she decided that all she could do was keep screaming and try to free herself.

"LET ME GO! LET ME GO!"

A moment later, the voices stopped as suddenly as they began and Priscilla fell to the ground. When she stood up, the kindly old woman whom she had met the day her family moved to town was standing before her. Priscilla noticed that she was dressed in the same long flowing black cape and carried the same walking stick.

"It's you," Priscilla said, wiping the dirt from her knees. "You were standing outside our house the day that we came to town. But, I didn't see you here a minute ago. Did you see what just happened?"

The woman with the kind face and gentle eyes smiled and nodded.

Out-of-the-blue, Priscilla remembered the library and looked at her watch. "Oh, my goodness! It's after ten."

She looked up at the woman, who continued to smile sweetly. "It was nice seeing you again, but I have to get to the library."

"You don't need to go to the library," the old woman said. "I have the information that you seek."

Priscilla welcomed the sound of the old woman's soft voice.

"What do you mean?" she asked, drawing a little bit closer.

The old woman removed her hood as she continued to speak. "A long time ago, a lovely young couple, the Samuels, moved into the house in which you now live. They had a sweet baby girl named Sarah. Sarah was beautiful, with blue eyes, blond hair, and the sweetest smile. In fact, she looked a lot like you."

Priscilla's eyes grew wider—she was eager to hear more.

"Her parents loved her very much, but sometimes found it hard to understand her ways. You see, she was a bit of a tomboy, just like you. But, she always carried a special doll that her grandmother had made for her."

Priscilla looked away and began to think about the strange doll that she found in the attic.

"I'm sorry to interrupt, but what did the doll look like?" The woman paused. "If I recall correctly, the doll looked like an old man dressed in white, wearing a gold earring," she said with a distant look in her eyes.

Priscilla felt her heart skip a beat. "That's the doll I found in the attic," she said to herself.

"Well, anyway," the woman continued in a gentle voice, "the Samuels were thrilled to be living in such a fine house, in such a fine town as Dunville. At that time, the house was radiant. Even on the inside, the house was always warm and seemed to glow with a light that only a loving family could create. Sarah treated the house like a person and called it Maggie."

"Maggie?"

The old woman paused for a moment. Her skin was turning pale, but she continued in a voice that was noticeably weaker and filled with sadness. "The Samuels were so happy, until one afternoon in June when everything changed."

"What happened?"

The old woman paused once more and pulled a tissue from a pocket in her cape. As she did, Priscilla noticed a small tattoo on her forearm. It looked like a bird flying into the sun.

"Sarah, who was 11 years old at the time, drowned. She and couple of her friends were on their way home from school when they stopped at a nearby pond. Sarah was not a good swimmer and should never have gone near it, but she was easily influenced by others," the old woman said as she wiped a tear from her eye. "The residents expressed their sympathies to the Samuels, but it did little to ease their pain."

Priscilla sat down on the curb.

The old woman's expression grew even more pitiful. "Now they had nothing left. Not even Sarah's beloved doll to remember her by. Even though many searched for it, it was never found."

Priscilla's stomach began to churn and her mind raced. "What's so special about the doll?" she asked timidly.

The old woman looked Priscilla straight in the eye and said, "Find the doll and you will find the power of the people."

Priscilla had no idea what the woman was talking about, but she wanted to yell, "Wait a minute, I have the doll."

"What a sad story," she said, instead.

"There's more," said the old woman. "After the death of Sarah, nothing in Dunville was the same. The Samuels, who were horribly grief stricken over the loss of their only child, blamed the whole town for what had happened. They also vowed to never make another repair to their house as long as they lived. They knew that since the town prided itself on its pristine appearance, this would be the perfect revenge."

"So that's why my house is the only run-down house in town."

The old woman nodded.

"The house, which had been bright and warm while Sarah was alive, grew cold and dark after she died. There was a constant chill which, I believe, represented the house's sadness over the loss of its beloved Sarah," she said, her voice little more than a whisper. "When the townspeople realized what was going on, they vowed to shun the Samuels, or cut them off from the town until they made the necessary repairs to their house. Standing behind their decision, the Samuels lived in Dunville for years in total seclusion. Then, one day, they simply disappeared."

"So, that's why the townspeople treat us like they do," Priscilla said, kicking a bunch of pebbles into the storm drain. "It's because of how the house looks."

When the old woman did not answer, Priscilla turned around. Standing hunched over, leaning on her walking stick, the old woman looked awfully tired.

"There's something that I need to know," Priscilla whispered as she watched an ant zigzag across the blacktop. "Strange things have been happening in the house—magical things. Could my house be magical?"

Once again, the old woman did not answer. Priscilla stood up and looked around, but she was gone.

"Hello—ma'am? Where did you go? I didn't even get your name," cried Priscilla, lowering her head. Then, slowly, a smile broke across her face when she realized that the old woman had scratched her name into the dirt.

On her way home, Priscilla could not stop repeating: *Mrs. Willowby, Mrs. Willowby, Mrs. Willowby . . .*

This has been the most amazing day, she thought as she crossed Jackson Street. *I didn't expect that getting the information I needed would be this easy.*

She thought about all the weird things that had happened to her since she moved to Dunville. She had been right about everything—her crazy neighbors, the doll from the attic, and her house. It *had* been trying to communicate with her. It *wanted* her to find the doll—but *why?*

Crossing her lawn, she also thought about what she was going to tell her mother and sister. Without proof that her story was true, she was sure her family would accuse her of lying. After all, she did have an active imagination and a tendency to exaggerate.

When she got inside, she raced up the stairs to her bedroom and took Sarah's doll from the shelf over her bed. Lying down, she looked at the little doll. She studied the paint on his face, the materials used to make his hair, the fabric used to make his clothing, and his tiny gold earring.

I don't see anything special about him, she thought as she placed the doll down next to her on her pillow and took a nap.

Later that evening, she decided to have a talk with her mother. After brushing her teeth, she made her way down the long hallway towards her mother's bedroom. She hesitated for a moment, trying to choose her words. *"Knock, knock, knock,"* she gently tapped on the rough wooden door.

"Come on in," Mom called.

"Mom, can I talk to you about something?" Priscilla asked, standing in the doorway.

Mom was lying in bed reading. "Sure, come on in. Is anything wrong?"

Priscilla sat on the bed. "No, I just wanted to ask you something."

"Ask away," Mom said, smiling, as she put down her book.

Priscilla paused for a minute. "Why did you choose this house?"

Mom paused, too. "Well, I already told you that when I first saw this house, I knew that it was the one."

"Yeah, I know. But, *how* did you know?"

"What's this all about?"

Priscilla did not answer right away. She thought about that day in the attic, the whispers, and Mrs. Willowby. *I can't say anything yet,* she silently told herself.

Mom sighed and put down her book. "Listen, Priscilla, I know that this house isn't perfect, but we'll fix it up."

Priscilla felt like she was going to burst. Something told her that she needed to be honest with her mother.

"Mom, I have to tell you some things about this house," began Priscilla as she told her mother about Maggie, the whispers, and what happened in the attic. She also told her about Mrs. Willowby, the Samuels, and the doll.

"I've studied the doll about a dozen times, but I don't see what makes it special," she said.

"Maybe if you give it time, the answer will just come. Don't worry . . . you'll see. But, as far as the house goes, it's all so amazing. When I bought this house, I knew that it was special, but I had no idea that it was *enchanted.*"

"Enchanted? Does that mean that our house is magical?"

"Maybe . . . or, it could be haunted," Mom replied and giggled.

Priscilla scrunched up her face.

"Lighten up, Priscilla—I'm only kidding," Mom said as she motioned for her to move closer. "Priscilla—I have to tell you something. Maybe it will help you to understand what has happened here."

Mom's tone was very serious and Priscilla was anxious to hear what she had to say.

"I believe that some people are more sensitive than others to the forces of nature. For instance, some people know that it's going to rain before it actually does by the smell of the air, while others can sense impending illnesses by looking into a person's eyes. When I saw this house for the first time, it spoke to me."

"Really!" said Priscilla, her eyes widening.

"Well, no, not really. But, I felt drawn to the house. And the first time I set foot in it, I felt a special energy, or presence. And sometimes, in very rare circumstances, the place or object that embodies this energy can be drawn to a person who possesses this sensitivity, or second sense."

Priscilla started to tremble. *I must have this power of second sense too*, she thought to herself.

As if reading her mind, Mom said, "Maybe you have the second sense, too. That would explain why the house is communicating with you."

"That and the fact that I remind the house of Sarah."

Mom smiled. "I'm glad that you finally told me about all of this. We really need to stick together."

"I'm glad, too. It's good to know that I'm not going crazy."

Mom smiled, kissed her daughter on the forehead, and wished her a "good night".

Back in her room, Priscilla got ready for bed. As she pulled a nightshirt over her head, she felt great. She was happy to finally have the answers to some big questions.

"I knew that something was going on around here, Tikki. I'm *not* crazy . . . I actually feel kind of *empowered*," she said to her bird before slipping into bed.

Tikki, who was always an attentive listener, blinked, chirped twice, and closed her eyes.

The room was too hot to snuggle under the comforter, so Priscilla kicked it to the foot of the bed. As she tried to fall asleep, images of Maggie flashed in her head. *How wonderful it was to have a house like her—a house that had helped to bring her and her sister closer together.*

Priscilla was so grateful for Maggie's friendship that she felt she should do something to show her how much she was appreciated. It didn't take long to get an idea. It was perfect—she would make Maggie a part of her family.

She got out of bed, spread a blanket on the floor, and sat down next to Tikki's cage. She wanted to be as close to her house as she could.

"Thank you for leading me to Sarah's doll and for helping to bring Penelope and me closer. I know that you have been sad for a long time, but you don't have to be sad any more. We can be your family, Maggie," Priscilla said as she glanced around at the walls and ceiling. "I wonder if Maggie is short for Margaret. I've always loved that name. Well, Maggie—I think that Sarah must have loved you a lot to give you such a pretty name."

While Priscilla waited for Maggie to reply, she noticed that Tikki was acting very strange. "Hey, what's wrong girl?" she said softly and opened the cage door.

Tikki, who had been making gurgling sounds like water going down a drain, backed away when Priscilla's hand approached.

"It's okay, I'm not going to hurt you," she said as she tried to grab the bird. "Ouch!" she cried after Tikki bit her finger. She quickly withdrew her hand from the cage and slammed the wire door shut.

I hope she's not sick, she thought to herself as she wrapped herself up in her blanket.

When no reply from Maggie came, she fell asleep.

It seemed like she had just laid her head down when she was awakened by Tikki's screeching. Looking up at her walls, she rubbed her eyes. "I can't believe what I'm seeing," she said to herself as she watched the calming blue color of her newly painted walls intensify to a bold electric blue.

"What's going on?"

Trembling, she pulled Tikki's cage close to her and pulled her blanket up over the two of them. From under the blanket, she could feel the air inside the room begin to stir. She lifted the blanket in time to see the air whip itself up into a mini cyclone. Dirty clothes from the floor, books, CDs, and even dust were carried up towards the ceiling. She was afraid that she and Tikki would be next but, as the minutes passed, they remained untouched.

The whirring sound of the cyclone, along with the banging of the books and CDs against the walls, became almost too much for Priscilla to bear. She covered her ears and began to shout, **"Whoever's doing this please make it stop!"** Tikki was screeching even louder and Priscilla wished that she could somehow comfort her. A few seconds later, the noise stopped and Priscilla felt something land on her head. From under her blanket, she reached out her hand and grabbed at the object. "Gotcha!" she said, pulling a pair of jeans and an orange baseball cap into her lap.

Feeling silly, she slowly peeked out from under her blanket. The stillness of the room felt strange. Tikki had stopped screeching and now it seemed a little too quiet. When she tried to stand, the floor started to shake, and the wind outside began to howl.

"This has to be a dream," she said to herself as she ran over to the bed, leaving Tikki behind.

Frightened, she jumped onto it, and the floor's rumbling stopped. She closed her eyes and took a deep breath. "Let it be over . . . let it all be over," she chanted.

She opened her eyes in time to see tiny rays of white light emerging from her walls. The light started dimly, but began to intensify until the whole room was filled with a warm glowing light. It reminded Priscilla of the light in the attic. She tried to convince herself that she wasn't afraid, and slid down from the bed.

Like warm breezes that caress the skin on a summer day, the walls began to speak: "Magnificent is my name."

Priscilla stood next to the bed unsure what to do. She began to feel words forming in her throat. "I see—Maggie is short for Magnificent," she said, her voice quivering.

The walls responded by growing brighter.

Overcome with feelings of love and friendship, Priscilla walked over to the wall and gently placed her hand upon it. She felt a warm, pleasant sensation surge from the tips of her fingers through her arms, and down to her toes. *This must be what love feels like.*

She remembered what Mrs. Willowby said about the warmth meaning that the house was happy.

"I'm glad that you're happy, Maggie. We can take care of each other now."

Chapter Eight

Penelope Rejects the Existence of Magic

*T*he next morning, Penelope sat at the kitchen table nibbling on a dry piece of toast. She couldn't stop thinking about what her sister had told her about the mysterious woman wearing the black cape. *Whispering winds and women who appear out of nowhere—Priscilla's imagination is definitely working overtime.*

A moment later, Mom shuffled into the kitchen and sat down next to her daughter.

"Good morning, sleepyhead. You've been sleeping in a lot lately. School starts soon, so you're going to have to start getting up earlier."

"I know, I know, but I've been so tired lately."

"Me too," Priscilla said as she sleepily walked in and plopped down in the chair next to her sister.

"Why are you so tired?" Penelope asked.

"Are you having trouble sleeping too?" inquired Mom.

"Well, actually, something really amazing happened in my room last night," Priscilla replied, timidly.

Mom and Penelope stared at her.

"What happened?" asked Mom in an anxious voice.

Priscilla told them everything that occurred the night before. When she was done, Penelope started to laugh. "Do you really expect us to believe that ridiculous story?"

Mom gave Penelope a harsh look. "Don't be so quick to judge your sister. I believe her."

Penelope's mouth fell open. "Since when?"

Priscilla and Mom smiled at each other and Mom changed the subject. "School starts soon, you know. How would you like to go to the mall today? I don't have to work, and you both need some school clothes."

While waiting for her daughters' reply, Mom grabbed a cup of coffee.

Penelope's face lit up at the mention of new clothes. "Sure, that sounds good. I'll finish eating and get ready."

"I guess I could use some new sneakers," Priscilla added.

An hour later, Mom yelled up the stairs. **"Hey guys, it's almost eleven o'clock. We really should get going!"**

"I'm ready to go," Penelope answered as she came down the stairs.

"I'm ready too," Priscilla said as she ran down the stairs, passing her sister. "I had trouble finding a clean pair of socks."

"From what I can see, you managed. Wait for me in the car. Okay? I must have left my keys in the kitchen," Mom said as she ushered the girls towards the door.

Outside, Penelope and Priscilla were surprised to see a crowd of people gathered on the sidewalk in front of their house, smiling and pointing at something. Penelope called to her mother who was still inside, "Mom! Hurry and come out here. A bunch of our neighbors are here, and they're staring at our house—and they're smiling!"

"What's the matter?" Mom asked, visibly concerned, as she joined her daughters who were now standing on the sidewalk with the neighbors.

"Look!" Priscilla said as she gasped and pointed up at the house. "It's incredible!"

The house, which had been run-down and tired-looking for so long, had somehow been restored to its original splendor overnight. From its vibrant blue with white trimmed exterior, to its magnificent stained glass windows, the house was by far the most beautiful house in the whole town.

"I can't believe it," Mom said, walking over to the porch and running her hand over the shiny smooth white railing. "How could this have happened?"

Penelope could not take her eyes off the house as she made her way over to where her mother and sister were standing. Part of her wished she were dreaming because then she would not have to make sense out of what she was seeing. But, another part of her was glad to see the change, no matter how it happened. She decided to reserve an opinion until she heard what her mother had to say.

"Mom, how do you think this happened?"

Mom looked dumbfounded. She took a deep breath and turned to her daughter. "I know that you don't believe in magic Penelope, but what else could it be?"

Not you too, Penelope thought.

"Of course . . . that's what I was going to say," Priscilla announced smiling. "You certainly can't deny what you can see with your own eyes."

Penelope folded her arms in front of her. "There has to be another explanation." She thought for a moment and turned to the townspeople. "Hello, my name is Penelope Post. I was just wondering if any of you caught a look at the workers before they left here this morning."

The neighbors stopped chatting, and a tall slender woman wearing a gray business suit and beige heels stepped forward. "Why no, we didn't," she said. "But, I have to say, whomever you used did a great job—boy did they work quickly."

Mom, Penelope, and Priscilla looked at each other.

"We're the Posts. What can we do for you," Mom said suddenly.

"I noticed the house on my way to work and I just had to stop. And—since I'm here—I'd like to welcome you to the neighborhood," said the woman in the beige heels.

"Thank you," Mom said as she gave her girls a curious look.

Suddenly, the whole crowd came up on the lawn.

"Hi, I'm your neighbor, Al Stevens," said a kind-looking man with wavy silver hair and dimples. "Welcome to the neighborhood." He offered his hand to Mom and she hesitantly accepted it.

"Hello."

"Welcome to the neighborhood," said another man wearing a black business suit and an orange tie. "We would like to apologize for our behavior since you arrived. We're really not bad people, we were just afraid."

"Afraid of what?" Mom asked with a puzzled look.

The girls looked at each other.

"Well, to be honest, we thought that your family had come here to hurt us," continued the man.

"*Us*, hurt *you*?" Penelope asked in disbelief.

"What are you talking about?" asked Mom, her left eyebrow raised

The man did not answer, but a short woman in a bright yellow pantsuit stepped forward. "Hello, Mrs. Post. My name is Sandy Peterson," the woman said in a soft child-like voice. "Welcome to Dunville."

Mom looked like an animal caught in a trap. "Thank you."

"I hate to be the one to tell you this, but before you moved here your neighbor, Mrs. Maven, spread some stories about your family."

Mom gasped. "What *sort* of stories?"

"Well, she went around telling everyone that she knew of your family and that you were terrible, sloppy people. At first no one believed her because she drinks and all. But after we saw your old car pull into town, we changed our minds."

"You thought badly of us and decided to believe rumors because of our *car*!"

Sandy Peterson smiled and showed the most perfect white teeth. "Well, not just your car, but your overall appearance. You see, Mrs. Post, in Dunville we measure our strength as a community by our town's overall appearance. Uniformity and cleanliness are the foundations for success, you know. That is why we always dress in our best clothes and always keep our homes neat and clean. It has been our way of life for hundreds of years and our proof is in the hundreds of clean, proper, and happy people who live here."

Mom pulled her girls closer to her.

The man with the wavy silver hair continued. "You need to understand that we're only trying to protect our traditions. In the past, we have had trouble with people who have threatened our way of life. People like the Samuels, who used to live in your house. Mrs. Maven convinced us that you were related to them and had come to bring us down."

"I assure you that we are not related to the Samuels, and we have never had any intentions of hurting anyone. We only wanted to make a new home for ourselves," said Mom.

Penelope started to worry. "Mom . . . I'm scared. Who are the Samuels?"

"We'll talk about it later," Mom said as she turned to face her neighbors. "Thank you for stopping by. It was nice to meet all of you, but we really have to be going now."

She turned around and headed towards the driveway. "Let's go girls!"

Penelope and Priscilla followed their mother.

Unexpectedly, Sandy Peterson shouted, "**Wait...Mrs. Post!**" and began to waddle towards them. "I have something of great importance to talk to you about."

Mom ignored the woman, and she and the girls got into the car quickly, and locked the doors.

"I'm head of the PTA," she continued, almost completely out of breath, and then threw herself on the hood of the car.

"What is she *doing*?" Priscilla asked, giggling.

"Stop that, Priscilla," Mom snapped. "She could be dangerous."

Priscilla continued to giggle. "I doubt it."

Sandy Peterson peeled herself from the hood of the car and headed around to the driver's side window. "Please wait. I hope that you'll come to our first meeting in September." Her face was now pressed up against the window.

"This is ridiculous," Mom said as she rolled down her window. "Ms. Peterson, I'll have to see."

"Well, you simply *must* come. The meetings are held on the first Friday of every month at my house. We would really like you to be there."

"Really, Ms. Peterson, I'll let you know."

It was obvious to Penelope that her mother was trying to keep her cool.

"We really need to go now. Thanks for stopping by."

Mom waved to the crowd before she put the car in reverse. As she slowly rolled out of the driveway, Ms. Peterson began to shout: **"How about if I put you down anyway. If there is a problem, you can call me. My number is in the book."**

As the tires of the car hit the end of the driveway, the brakes let out the loudest squeal and the car came to a sudden stop. Penelope watched as her mother got out of the car slowly. Eager to hear every word that was being said, she rolled down her window. She had never seen her mother look so angry.

"Okay, let me be honest with you, Ms. Peterson. I really have no desire to join the PTA, or any other organization at this time. I am way too busy right now. And furthermore, I don't appreciate being pushed like this. You people don't talk to us for all this time and, when you finally do, your biggest concern is the PTA?"

Penelope could not believe her ears. Her mother had never talked to anyone that way before.

"Mom, are you all right?" she asked, as she looked at her neighbors who were appeared stunned by her mother's outburst.

Mom ran her fingers through her thick brown hair—something she always did when she was under stress, and looked around at the crowd. "Yes, Penelope, I'm all right. I'm sorry everyone. I don't know what's gotten into me. I guess I'm just feeling a little anxious these days. So much has happened in such a short time."

"We understand. You've been very busy around here, and we really appreciate it," said Sandy. "I'll give you a call in a couple of days."

"That would be great," Mom agreed with a smile.

As the car pulled out of the driveway, Penelope could hear the neighbors shouting, "The house looks wonderful! I love the color . . . it really complements the other houses in the neighborhood!"

For the first time in a long time, Penelope started to have faith in her sister. *Everything that she's told me about this town is true. But there is one thing that I can't figure out—how did the house restore itself? It's unbelievable —there must be a rational explanation,* she thought as she turned around in her seat and watched her neighbors walk away.

As Mom drove through town towards the highway, Penelope could feel the tension inside the car. "Are we still going to the mall?" she asked.

"No!" said Mom.

"Then, where are we going?"

"I had to get out of there. I thought that a drive would do us all a lot of good."

Priscilla, who had not said a word since Mom pulled out of the driveway, spoke: "Don't you think that we should talk about what happened back there? Aren't either of you the least bit curious how the house became restored?"

Mom sighed. "Let's talk about it later. I just want to drive," she replied, staring out at the highway stretching before her.

An hour later, Mom pulled into their driveway. "Come on girls, let's have something to eat."

In the car, Penelope sat slumped against the torn, blue vinyl seat. She had spent the whole ride thinking about the fact that she did not get to the mall. "Mom . . . when are we going to get my new clothes?" she whined from the back seat.

Mom got out of the car. "Maybe tomorrow. Hopefully, after a good night's sleep, the world will make more sense."

That night at dinner, Penelope looked around the kitchen. It was amazing—the cracks in the walls were gone, and the pipes weren't making those banging noises. As she plopped another spoonful of mashed potatoes onto her plate she wondered: *How did all of this happen?*

Mom, who earlier appeared to be experiencing some kind of breakdown, now seemed calm and cheerful.

"Girls, isn't all of this wonderful. I can't explain any of it, but we have a new house. I just can't believe it . . . and the neighbors are talking to us. Things can't get much better than this."

"But Mom, aren't you the least bit curious about how the house was restored?" asked Penelope.

"Of course I am. But there's nothing that I can do about it tonight. In time, the answers will come."

Penelope scrunched up her face. "That's it—that's all you have to say!"

"Maybe it was magic," Priscilla said suddenly from across the table.

"Here we go again. When are you going to stop harping on all of that? I admit that you might have been right about our neighbors, but. . . "

Mom shot Penelope a look of disapproval. "Don't be so quick to judge things."

For Mom's sake, Penelope agreed to keep an open mind.

When everyone was finished eating, Penelope offered to clear the dishes. As she stood up, she noticed something move outside the kitchen window. "Hey, Mom! I see something outside in our bushes," she said as she got up and went over to the long, narrow window next to the pantry.

Mom and Priscilla followed.

"**Look! There it goes**," Priscilla shouted.

In the moonlight, the three could see a large shadowy figure waddling away from the house.

"Whoever it is, they have a limp," said Mom.

"Didn't Mrs. Maven have a limp?" Priscilla asked.

"Yes, I believe she did," answered Mom. "But why would Mrs. Maven want to spy on us?"

"I don't know, but I think that Priscilla is right. Mrs. Maven did limp," said Penelope.

"Well, whoever it was, they're in need of some serious psychological help. Imagine that . . . trying to peek in decent people's windows. No matter—I will go out tomorrow and pick up some heavier curtains," Mom said as she began to clear away the dinner plates.

That night, Penelope had a strange dream. She was back in the city, in her favorite store in the mall, *Le Petite Chic,* when she ran into Jasmine.

"Hi, Jasmine! I didn't know that you shopped here, too."

Jasmine looked strange. Her eyes were black and her mouth was gone.

"What's wrong with you Jasmine? Why won't you talk to me? I thought you were my friend," Penelope cried as she grabbed her friend's shoulders and shook her.

Jasmine broke free from Penelope's grasp and walked, zombie-like, out of the store and into the mall. Penelope ran after her with tears in her eyes. "**Mouth or no mouth, real friends stick together**," she shouted.

Once inside the mall, Penelope no longer saw Jasmine, or any one else for that matter. The mall was completely empty and the only sound that she could hear was the *clip-clop* noises from her shoes as they echoed through the cavernous building. It reminded her of the caves she had seen on television.

"What's going on here? This can't be happening," she said to herself as she began to run—frantically searching for the people who occupied these places just a few minutes earlier.

Running past the mall information desk, she saw a large blue neon sign which read, "You're late . . . but there's still time."

When she found herself walking down the dark hallway of her old school, she wondered: *Late for what?*

Suddenly she heard . . . chimes, like the chimes that had hung on the porch of her old house.

"What am I doing here?" she asked herself as she noticed a light coming from one of the classrooms.

Going inside, she was surprised to see her sister sitting alone at the front of the room, and she was wearing a sparkling blue dress and black patent leather shoes.

"What are you doing here?" Penelope inquired.

Priscilla smiled. "I'm here for school, just like you."

"But why are you dressed like that?"

"What do you mean? You know that this dress is my favorite."

Confused, Penelope ran out of the room.

"It's not too late. . ." Priscilla yelled after her.

In the hallway, she ran into Jasmine again, but this time she was herself.

"Where are you running to?" Jasmine asked.

Penelope felt as if she was going to cry. "I have to get out of here," she said and continued to run.

"There's still time. . . " Jasmine's voice trailed behind her like the tail of a kite.

When Penelope awoke, it was still dark outside and she was lying on her bedroom floor. Her blanket was wrapped around her, and her pillow was wedged under her head. *What a dream! That was freaky,* she thought to herself as she gathered up her things and climbed back into bed.

Right before she drifted off to sleep, she mumbled, "It's not too late. . ."

Chapter Nine

Priscilla's New Friends

A few weeks passed and it was the morning of the first day of school. At eight-fifteen, Priscilla sat down in the parlor and waited for her sister to come downstairs. Feeling a lot less nervous than she thought she would be, she looked over her class schedule. It was going to be strange not being in the same class as her sister.

Doodling on the cover of her new notebook, she drew a figure that looked like a bird. It reminded her of the bird tattoo on Mrs. Willowby's arm and she wondered if she would ever find out who Mrs. Willowby really was.

Moments later, the sound of Penelope's voice pierced the veil of silence that hung over the parlor. "I'm ready," she announced, strutting into the room.

She was wearing a pair of tight, low cut jeans and a tiny pink metallic top that showed her belly button. Priscilla gasped at the sight of her sister's bare stomach.

"What have you done now?" she said, trying not to sound too disgusted. "And what did you do to your hair? It looks like a pink bird's nest."

Penelope's pink hair was pulled up into a messy ponytail that was held together by some sort of clip that sprouted delicate pink, green and blue feathers into the air in a fan shape. To complete the look, thin strands of pink hair danced around her face.

Penelope glared at her sister. "What do you think I did?" I dyed it last night."

Priscilla glared back. "But why did you choose pink?"

"My hair is not pink, it's fuchsia. And this is the latest thing in hair jewelry—a Blossoming Peacock," she added, pointing to her clip.

Priscilla was not impressed. "You know, if Mom was here, she would never let you leave the house looking like that."

Penelope ignored her sister. "Let's go! I don't want to be late," she said as she grabbed her purple backpack and headed for the door.

Priscilla grabbed her grass-green backpack and followed.

Outside, the sky was clear and the air was warm. It was the first time they had ever walked to school. In the city, their mother had always driven them.

"I wonder what the other kids will be like," Penelope said as the two approached Second Avenue.

Priscilla didn't hear her sister. She was thinking about her mother. *I wish that Mom hadn't been called into work. I know that she really wanted to take us to school today.*

A moment later, Penelope stopped. "What's wrong, Priscilla? You haven't said a word since we left home."

Priscilla dropped her backpack to the ground. "Uh . . .I just don't like the idea of having to walk through those creepy woods."

Running through the center of town, along Lincoln Avenue, was a narrow strip of woods called Nelson Woods. The woods divided the town into two sections: the north side, and the south side. The Posts lived on the north side, and the school was on the south side, so the girls would have to brave the woods in order to get there.

"Don't worry, you're not alone—and besides, there is nothing to be afraid of."

"I'm not afraid . . . I just don't like the woods, that's all."

As the girls stood at the edge of Nelson Woods, they glanced around. Priscilla watched as squirrels chased each other from tree to tree and birds fluttered around them. On the ground, forest ferns and wild flowers swayed in the gentle breeze. Following the well-worn dirt path before her, Penelope led the way. The two carefully stepped over fallen branches and ruts in the ground as they approached Fisherman's Friend Pond.

Dunville Elementary School was now visible through the trees, but they still had a distance to walk. Priscilla's stomach started to do flip-flops as she thought about all the unfamiliar faces that she was about to encounter. She dreaded the thought of making new friends.

Once inside the school, though, her butterflies were calmed by the familiar smells of chalk and new paper. And, to her surprise, it was Penelope who now looked pale and disoriented.

"Are you all right Penelope?"

"Yeah, I'll be fine once I find my classroom."

Priscilla pointed to a small sign on a classroom door. "Isn't that it—number *215*?"

Penelope gave her sister an uneasy look. "Yeah, thanks. I'll see you later."

As Priscilla searched for her homeroom, she hoped that her sister would be okay. A moment later, she found classroom *210*. Glancing over her shoulder before going in, she hoped to see her sister one last time. Instead, she saw Jasmine heading towards room *215*. Penelope greeted her in the doorway, and the two hugged and quickly engaged in conversation. Priscilla could feel her body tense up and the butterflies return. But, she couldn't worry about them right now—she needed to focus on herself.

Walking into her homeroom, her eyes were fixed on the floor's shiny pale ivory and beige tiles. At the back of the room, she took a seat behind a chubby boy with greasy-looking blonde hair. The confidence she had gained recently began to waver as each student entered the classroom. Suddenly, chimes sounded and everyone sat down. She wondered if it was the homeroom bell and, if it was, where was her teacher? A moment later, a tiny hairless man walked briskly into the classroom. "Hello, my name is Mr. Krumple—with a *K*."

After dropping an overflowing brown leather duffel bag onto his desk, the little man scratched his name on the clean blackboard. "Repeat after me," he said waving his wooden pointer. "Mr. Krumple."

"Mr. Krumple," repeated the class.

When Mr. Krumple spoke, the words seemed to sputter out of his mouth, like the exhaust of a tired old car. But, there was something about the way that he sputtered and used his pointer that led Priscilla to believe that he would not be a pushover.

"I'd like to . . . introduce a new student . . . Ms. Priscilla . . . Post," he said as his tiny gold-rimmed glasses slid to the end of his stubby little nose.

Priscilla tried to hide behind the greasy-haired boy.

"Stand up, Priscilla, and tell us a little bit about yourself," Mr. Krumple said as he stood in front of her desk and whipped his pointer in her face.

Priscilla, who had always been shy, hated speaking in public. This was her worst fear— the spotlight thrust upon her, even for a second. Looking around the room, she realized that it would be even more embarrassing if she just sat there. She could feel her lip start to quiver and her heart beat faster as she slowly rose from her chair. "Hi . . . my name is Priscilla Post. I moved here from Chicago a little over a month ago, and I live at *301* Jackson Street."

Then she paused, perhaps waiting for a reaction from her fellow students when they realized where she lived, but kept her eyes forward—planted on the colorful world map above the blackboard. Her mom had taught her that if she ever had to speak in public, she should keep her eyes on something calming. Even though the map was not exactly calming, it served to distract her from thinking about how nervous she was.

As she was about to continue, something else distracted her. From out of the corner of her eye, she could see a couple of girls whispering, two rows over. *Where they talking about her?*

When she finished speaking, Mr. Krumple once again waved his pointer in her face and she sat down. Glancing over at the two girls, she noticed that they were now quiet.

Ten minutes later, the chimes sounded again. Priscilla watched from her seat as the room quickly emptied. The only kids left were the two girls she had seen whispering. She turned away when she saw one of the girls, the one with skin the color of creamy coffee and braces on her teeth, coming towards her.

"Hi, I'm Melanie. I really like what you've done to your house," she said, enthusiastically.

Priscilla slowly turned around and smiled. "Thanks."

The other girl, who had curly red hair and freckles, appeared to be shy. "I . . . I . . . really like the shade of blue that you used," she said from across the room while she fiddled with the Velcro closure on her backpack.

"Thanks," replied Priscilla, her butterflies almost gone. "But, we really didn't do anything."

"How can you say that?" cried Melanie. "The whole town is raving about your house."

"The whole town knows about our house?"

"Sure . . . news travels fast around here," said Melanie. "Well . . . we have to go. We should sit together at lunch."

Priscilla smiled shyly. "I'd like that."

As she gathered up her things, she could not believe what had just happened. She had made some friends without the help of her sister. Everything was going to be okay.

Out in the hallway, she spotted Jasmine and her sister down the hall, near the lockers. As she watched the two of them talk, laugh, and hang on each other, a dull pain throbbed in the pit of her stomach. She couldn't help but think about how close she and her sister used to be, and tears formed in her eyes. If it weren't for Jasmine maybe they could be again.

As she searched for her locker, she realized that it was right next to Jasmine's.

"Great! Now how am I supposed to avoid her?"

She quickly decided that making a scene would be immature, so she quietly approached her locker, hoping to go unnoticed. Suddenly, she felt like she was going to be sick. *I've got to get out of here,* she thought as she turned around and ran down the hall towards the gym.

Later that day at home, Mom was sitting on the front porch. As the girls approached, Priscilla watched as her mother's smile turned into a frown.

"Penelope—what have you done to your hair?" she cried.

"Can we talk about that later? I want to tell you about my day."

"No, young lady, I think that we should talk about it now!"

Priscilla dropped her backpack and sat down next to Mom. "Yeah, Penelope—we'd like to talk about it now," she said, giggling.

Mom shot Priscilla a look of disapproval. "Maybe you're right Penelope. I think that we should talk about it later—in private. But, until then, you might as well tell me about your day. How was it?"

Penelope's eyes lit up. "Well . . . since you asked, it was great!" "I mostly hung around with Jasmine. She's great!

I can learn a lot from her . . . and she introduced me to a lot of other kids."

Mom tried to smile. "I'm glad to hear that it went well."

Mom turned to Priscilla. "And, what about you? How was your first day of school?"

Priscilla stood up. "It was better than I thought it would be. I made a couple of new friends, too."

"That's wonderful. See, I told you that everything would be okay."

Priscilla smiled and went into the house leaving Mom and Penelope alone to have their private discussion.

Right before bed, she sat in the fireplace room talking to Maggie. "What I really wanted to tell Mom this afternoon was that even though I made a couple of new friends, I still miss Penelope. I'm afraid that I'm going to lose her to Jasmine. I can feel her slipping away again. Please talk to me Maggie."

A few minutes later, Priscilla smiled when she heard Maggie's voice. She came to her in her usual way—whispers like the wind, wrapping around Priscilla like a soft blanket.

"My friend. . . don't fear. Magic is in the air. Magic is the key."

"What do you mean? I don't understand."

"Be patient and have faith in yourself and your sister. In time, the answers will come to you."

"But Maggie, what do you mean by that?" Priscilla wailed, displeased with her friend's answer.

After awhile, when Maggie failed to respond to Priscilla's cry for help, she ran to her room, upset, and plopped down on her bed. She could not help but feel that her friend let her down. She tried to make sense of what Maggie had said, but could not.

"I don't want to be patient," she said to herself. "Maybe if I ask her again, she'll tell me what I need to know."

She sat up on her bed and called to Maggie. "Please Maggie talk to me again. Please give me a sign that things are going to get better."

The room was quiet and the wind still. Maggie did not return that evening.

Fall passed quickly and the family settled into a comfortable routine. Winter came to Dunville and the quiet town became even quieter. With the snow came closings of many of the town's businesses, and all of its schools.

Despite the harsh winter, life was pretty good for the Posts. They had not seen or heard from Mrs. Maven in weeks, and the girls were doing well in school. Priscilla was on the girl's basketball team, and Penelope was a part of the most popular group of kids

The day after New Year's day, children were due back at school following the long winter break. Standing outside her house alone, Priscilla looked down and saw that her boots were covered in yet another layer of new snow—she sighed. *What kind of break from winter was it anyway?* she thought as she crossed Jackson Street.

Penelope, who had been as healthy as a rosy-cheeked baby during the entire break, had suddenly come down with the flu. *How convenient,* Priscilla thought. *I bet she planned the whole thing.*

When Mom came to her the night before to tell her that she would be walking to school by herself in the morning, Priscilla told her that she didn't mind. Actually, she had welcomed a break from listening to her sister go on and on about Jasmine.

Crunching along in her black rubber boots, she tried not to worry about walking through Nelson Woods alone.

"I can do this," she said to herself as she approached the woods. "I don't need Penelope."

Standing at the edge of the woods, she noticed that the landscape before her looked like one large tangled mass of frozen trees and brush. Glancing down at the ground, she searched for the path, but it was gone—erased by the thick blanket of snow. The wind was howling fiercely, echoing through the trees like a lost wolf searching for its pack.

"There's no reason to be afraid," she said to herself as she forced her feet forward. "Anything capable of doing me harm would not be out in this weather."

Pulling her collar up around her ears, she plodded through the snow. About halfway through the woods, she heard the sound of snow crunching. She stopped and cautiously looked around. "Who's there?" she called out

When no one answered, she continued on, quickening her pace. Her breath looked like the exhaust from an old steam engine as it escaped in plumes that trailed behind her. Overhead the branches of trees covered with ice made a *clinking* sound as they danced and bumped into each other in the wind. Those trees that still wore a blanket of fresh snow were rapidly undressing under the winds direction.

Nearing Fisherman's Friend Pond, she heard the crunching sound again. Once again she stopped, feeling more frightened than before. **"I HEAR YOU! SHOW YOURSELF!"**

Suddenly, Mrs. Maven leapt out from behind a huge tree trunk and grabbed Priscilla around the waist.

"NO! WHAT ARE YOU DOING?" Priscilla screamed as she kicked at the old woman's legs.

"Don't fight me! It will do no good," Mrs. Maven said as she pinned Priscilla to a nearby tree.

More frightened than she had ever been in her whole life, she did not move. She wanted to scream again, but she knew no one would hear her.

"Let me go you crazy old kook," she managed to say.

Mrs. Maven did not say a word, but breathed heavily on Priscilla, forcing her to inhale the stinging aroma of alcohol that saturated her breath.

"I've been watching you—you and your family," Mrs. Maven slurred her words as she pushed Priscilla harder against the tree.

Priscilla could not scream because she was having trouble breathing, but she could feel the frozen tree bark, sharp like giant rosebush thorns, poking through her jacket.

"What do you want?" she managed to ask.

Mrs. Maven stepped back for a moment and then put her face right up against Priscilla's.

"I want to expose your family for what it is," she said, spitting. "Then maybe this town will take me seriously. I've been the town joke for enough years. It's all going to end soon."

With the majority of Mrs. Maven's weight off her chest, Priscilla was once again able to take full breaths. But, after inhaling the woman's hot, heavy breath, she wished to be breathless again.

"I don't know what you're talking about."

Again, Mrs. Maven pushed Priscilla up against the tree—this time even harder.

"What do you think we are?" she gasped, trying to force the woman off her.

Mrs. Maven stood up straight, and Priscilla watched her thick lips as she spoke. "*Witches,* of course."

"*Witches?*" Priscilla repeated, her eyebrows peaking.

"Yes."

Priscilla stood up tall. **"We're not witches you old kook!"** she yelled, and with all her strength, pushed Mrs. Maven away.

The old woman tumbled backwards waving her arms in the air and then fell to the ground with a *thud*. Priscilla could not help but think that this was where the horrid old woman belonged since she was as wild as any animal in the woods.

Lying in the snow, Mrs. Maven was as motionless as a fallen tree. Priscilla wondered, suddenly, if she had done something terrible. *What if I killed her*, she thought and fell to her knees.

"Mrs. Maven . . . Mrs. Maven . . . are you okay?" she cried and gently patted her face.

When Mrs. Maven finally came around, she looked at Priscilla and smiled in a way that said: *How dare you try to hurt me.*

When she spoke, her eyes were as dark as night and as angry as frightened wasps. "That was a bold move little witch, but you are no match for me. You and your family may have fooled the others, but I'm not blind. I saw what happened to your house. That was the work of the devil," she spit and grabbed Priscilla's arm.

"She's crazy," Priscilla said to herself as she broke free from Mrs. Maven's grasp.

Her instinct was to run, but before her legs got the message, Mrs. Maven sprang up from the ground with amazing speed, grabbed her arm once again, and stared into her eyes. "Hey! You remind me of that Samuels' girl, the one that drowned years ago. She was a peculiar sort— that girl. I used to see her talking to herself. Her family was even worse, especially her mother. She had some strange ways—that one did."

Mrs. Maven paused. Her lips softened and her face grew pensive. With her eyes fixed on a point somewhere above Priscilla's head, she seemed to be in a trance. *What could she be thinking about?*

While the two stood still in the frozen woods in total silence, Priscilla took a good look at Mrs. Maven. Her hair was not pulled back, but was hanging freely, blowing in the wind like dusty cobwebs. She wore stained ruby red slacks, a dull green raincoat, and dirty, torn white tennis shoes. Priscilla realized, suddenly, that Mrs. Maven had relaxed her grip on her arm. If she acted quickly, maybe she could get away this time. However, as soon as she started to move, Mrs. Maven seemed to snap out of it.

"No matter how odd the Samuels were, at least they weren't witches!" she finally said, her face red and tense.

Frightened and worried that she had missed her last chance to flee, Priscilla began to cry.

Mrs. Maven laughed as her eyes widened. "What's the matter little girl? Can't you whip up a spell that will take you away from here?"

Not wanting to hear any more, Priscilla turned away and covered her ears. To her surprise, she heard a *meowing* sound that grew louder and louder. Glancing to her right, she saw Mrs. Maven's orange cat wander out from behind a Dogwood tree.

Mrs. Maven stopped and turned her attention to the cat. "Pumpkin, what are you doing out here? Did you follow mommy?" she slurred in a baby voice.

While Mrs. Maven was occupied with her cat, Priscilla ran as fast as she could towards the safety of her school. The remainder of her school day was a blur, as she found herself unable to concentrate. After all, a maniac was on the loose.

When she returned home after school, she ran up the stairs two steps at a time. She figured her sister would still be in bed and she had to tell her what had happened in the woods.

Bursting into her sister's room, Priscilla started rambling. "Penelope . . . you won't believe what happened to me today. That crazy old woman, Mrs. Maven, attacked me in the woods. She had me pinned to a tree, but then I broke free. She's insane—she called us witches," she said, now completely out of breath.

Penelope, who had three pillows wedged behind her head, and about a dozen magazines scattered all over her bedspread, sat straight up. "Whoa, whoa—wait a minute! Can't you see that I'm sick? You shouldn't just barge into a sick person's room like that!"

"Didn't you hear a word that I said?"

"Of course I did. But why are you so upset? You know that she's crazy . . . you said it yourself? After all, what harm can she really do?"

"I don't know. But, you should have seen the look on her face—it scared me."

Penelope didn't look at all concerned. "Enough about that . . . tell me something about school. Did anyone ask about me today? What was Jasmine wearing? Did she send any messages home for me?"

Priscilla bit her lip and exhaled loudly. "No . . . don't know . . . and no! You're so superficial! Is that stuff all that you care about?"

"No, of course not, but they're my friends."

"But I'm your sister. "Don't you care about me anymore? I could have been killed today!"

"Of course I care—I just don't understand you anymore, that's all. I mean . . . you're always going on and on about magic. And you weren't really hurt, were you? You really need to find a different hobby like I did."

"If you mean the hobby of imitating your friends, no thanks."

"Excuse me! What is that supposed to mean?"

"It means that you've changed. I don't even know you anymore. It's like you're a Jasmine clone or something."

"You know what . . . I think that you're jealous because I hang around with the popular kids, and you hang around with the basketball geeks."

With that said, Mom burst into the room. "Hey, hey—what's going on in here? I could hear you screaming from downstairs." Her eyes darted from daughter-to-daughter.

Turning to Priscilla she asked, "What are you doing in here? You know that your sister is sick. You shouldn't be upsetting her."

At that moment, Priscilla felt very alone. "I didn't mean to upset her. I was just telling her about what happened today in Nelson Woods."

Mom's angry expression softened a bit. "What happened?" she asked, visibly concerned.

Priscilla told her mother *everything* that happened in the woods that morning.

"I can't believe it! That woman should be in jail! I'm going to call the police!"

As Mom turned to go downstairs, Priscilla called to her. "Remember what happened last time we tried to call someone in town."

Mom stopped near the stairs and turned to face Priscilla. "I remember. But, we have to do something. What if she tries to hurt you again? She's a dangerous woman."

Priscilla sighed. "I know she is, but we'll just have to think of something on our own. It's the only way."

Mom managed a smile. "All right, honey, we'll try it your way for now, but I don't want either of you going anywhere alone, especially the woods."

Priscilla smiled and nodded.

"Do you understand Penelope?" Mom called from the stairs.

"Yes, Mom. I *get* it. Now will everyone please let me rest."

As Mom headed down the stairs, Priscilla hurried to her room.

On her floor, she knelt down next to Tikki's cage. "What's happening to my family, Tikki? Penelope and I never fought that way before," she said as she cautiously reached into the cage and lightly petted the bird's tiny head.

Tikki in turn quietly looked up at Priscilla and then let out a soft chirp.

"Thanks, Tikki . . . I'm glad that I have you to talk to."

She stood up and walked over to the window. "If I had the opportunity to have a real honest to goodness talk with Penelope, I would tell her a thing or two about how she's changed and how much I don't like her new look. I'd also tell her how phony I think her friends are." Tears welled up in Priscilla's eyes as she gazed out the window

Later that evening, her mood lightened as she lay on her bed thinking about her birthday party the following day and making a mental list of the gifts she had asked for. It was a family tradition to go to grandmother's house for dinner, followed by birthday cake for dessert, and then the opening of presents.

Priscilla could not wait to see her grandmother. The two had always been close, and even though her grandmother lived only three miles away in the next town, she had only seen her once since the move.

Later, on her way to the bathroom to brush her teeth, she heard voices coming from the foyer. Wondering who would be visiting at this late hour, she crept quietly over to the staircase and through the wooden spindles atop the stairs, she watched as Grandma and Mom stood in the foyer talking in hushed voices.

She wondered: *What is she doing here?*

Her eyes lit up and her impulse was to run down and greet her, but something inside her told her to wait. Then, a thought occurred to her. Her grandmother's poor eyesight usually prevented her from visiting in the evening. *Why had she risked coming over?*

Suddenly, Mom disappeared into the parlor and returned a moment later carrying a large cardboard box. Priscilla wondered: *What was in the box?* She strained to hear their whispered conversation but could not. It was all so mysterious.

When Mom fumbled with the box, Priscilla figured that it was heavy. Now, she was really curious about its contents. *Maybe it's my birthday present,* she thought. *But why did Grandma have to come over? Why didn't she just wait until tomorrow to give me her gift?*

Mom gave the box to Grandma and the two headed for the stairs. Priscilla could now hear what they were saying.

"Let's take the book to my room. The girls are in their rooms, so they won't hear us," Mom said.

Priscilla darted back to her room, where she waited until the voices had faded, and then tiptoed down the hall to her mother's door and stopped. She could hear Mom and Grandma talking.

"I've seen it coming for a while now," said Mom. "I wouldn't have called you if it wasn't important."

"Do you think they're ready?"

"Well, they are going to be 13 tomorrow. The book will teach them what they need to know."

So it's a "How-To" book, Priscilla thought to herself.

"Do you remember the day that you gave me the book?" Mom asked.

"Of course I do. You looked so confused . . . but with practice you eventually learned how to use it."

"I remember. But, it's been a long time since I've performed a spell, let alone opened the book."

"Did she just say *spell?*" Priscilla asked aloud.

"I know . . . the last time you worked a spell, you went into labor," Grandma said, chuckling.

"That was some day. I went from trying to turn a head of cabbage into a dinner for two, to lying in a hospital bed giving birth to twins, all in a matter of hours. I'll never forget that day."

"Neither will I."

The talking stopped, and all that Priscilla heard was the sound of rustling paper. "Just remember, when we open the book, do not read from its pages," Grandma said.

"Don't worry, I learned from your mistake. You didn't think I'd forget, did you?"

"One can hope, can't they?"

Mom began to giggle. "I could never forget my 16th birthday. As you were handing me the book, it fell on the floor and opened. You immediately began talking and waving your arms around. A second later, Dad's favorite chair went up in flames. What a coincidence it was that you hated that chair."

"Yes, it really was," said Grandma, her voice quivering. "You know how protective the book can be. If someone other than its new master reads from its pages, it will punish them by lashing out.

Mom smiled. "Well, just in case there's a danger of any further lashing out, I've hidden *my* favorite chair."

"Hey, wait a minute. I'm not the only one who used a spell to get what she wanted."

"I hope you're not trying to say that I abused my powers in the past. I was a good witch"

Priscilla could not believe her ears. *My mother and grandmother are talking about witchcraft,* she thought as she backed away from the door.

Quickly, she pulled herself together and returned to her place at the door. She had to know more. She could hear her grandmother saying…

"How could your forget about the time when you were 17 and you dried up the lake at the park because you wanted to find the ring you lost while throwing rocks with your friends? Sadly, all of the fish died and the mayor thought that it was the work of aliens from outer space."

Priscilla took a deep breath. She was glad that she decided to return to the door.

"Oh, yeah . . . I guess I forgot about that," Mom said in a voice just above a whisper.

Again, Priscilla strained to hear.

"Need I go on?" asked Grandma, the tone of her voice revealing her satisfaction with herself.

"Okay, I guess you're right. We've both done some things in the past that we're not proud of, but it will be our job to make sure the girls don't make the same mistakes. You have to admit that despite my rocky start, after a couple of years, I got really good."

"You're right Frances, you did become great. And with your guidance, the girls will be more powerful than anything we have ever seen."

"Do you really think so?"

"Yes, I do."

Priscilla's mouth fell open and she felt a chill go down her back.

"Why are you so sure?"

"The power of two, especially with twins, will be great."

"Why didn't you tell me this before?"

"I guess I just assumed that you knew."

Mom took a deep breath. "Maybe I did . . . maybe I always knew that they would be very powerful. I guess I never wanted to admit it because that would be like saying that a day will come when they won't need me anymore."

"Come on now . . . they'll always need their mother."

"I guess you're right. Enough talk . . . let's open the book. I want to take a look inside."

"Okay . . . here goes!"

Priscilla pressed her ear closer to the door, and when she no longer heard voices, she became alarmed. A little voice inside her told her that her mother and grandmother were in danger and, without hesitation, she slowly opened the door and poked her head in.

"Mom . . . Grandma . . . it's me, Priscilla. Can you hear me?" she whispered.

When neither Mom nor Grandma responded, she threw open the door and rushed into the room. Looking more closely at their faces, Priscilla realized they were frozen. Gazing around the room, she was alarmed to see a huge shimmering gray cloud hovering over her mother's dresser. *Is that what did this to them?* Priscilla wondered as the cloud began to move suddenly towards her.

Afraid of being swallowed up by the cloud beast and frozen, too, she dodged it and fled to a corner of the room, just feet away from Mom and Grandma.

"I have to get to them before it comes back around." As she watched the cloud turn around and move in her direction, she darted over to her mother and grabbed her wrist. *Thank goodness she's alive,* she thought as she took her grandmother's wrist and checked for her pulse. *They're both alive, but what do I do now?*

Looking over at the cloud that was almost upon them, she realized that there was nothing she could do for her family at that moment. As she raced back to the corner, she saw that the cloud had begun to grow, swallowing up the air around it. Priscilla began to panic. *What will happen to us if the cloud gets me?*

The cloud was now a little more than an arm's length away.

"**Go…Get away from me whatever you are!**" she shouted and punched at the shimmering gray mass. The cloud did not stop, but drew closer. Priscilla closed her eyes, inhaled deeply, and held it. She could feel the icy breath of the beast on her face, and she wondered what it would feel like to be frozen in a magical cloud. When nothing happened, she opened her eyes and saw the cloud float towards the door and then out into the hallway like a helium balloon being pulled by a restless child.

She exhaled loudly. "Thank goodness it's gone," she said to herself.

Curious to see where the cloud had gone, she peered out the door and watched as it danced down the hallway towards the back of the house. Along the way, it sprinkled its shimmering dust on everything in its path. As she stood there watching, she could not believe everything that was happening.

Once the cloud was out of sight, Priscilla returned to the bedroom where her mother and grandmother were still frozen in place.

Standing by her mother's side, she attempted to wake her. **"Please, Mom—wake up. It's me, Priscilla,"** she cried, shaking her mother.

Neither Mom nor Grandma responded.

"It's no use . . . I can't wake them," she cried as panic began to set in. "What can I do?" she asked aloud, staring at the book in her mother's arms. "Maybe the book will help me. It made this spell, so hopefully it can break it."

She tried to pry the book from her mother's arms, but could not. *I can't do this by myself,* she thought as she sat down on the bed.

Suddenly, the wind outside began to howl more fiercely than she had ever heard it before and the walls began to rumble.

"Is that you, Maggie? Oh, I hope that it's you. I need your help!"

Priscilla was right. Maggie had seen the cloud and had come to help. "Believe in the magic. The magic is the key."

Priscilla glanced around at the walls, which no longer glowed with bright, warm light—instead they possessed the dim light of a setting sun just before it disappears into the horizon.

"Is the book the magic that is supposed to help me?"

Maggie did not answer, but Priscilla watched as the book flew out of her mother's arms and landed on the floor.

Mom and Grandma began to stir.

"Thank goodness!" Priscilla said to herself and looked up at the ceiling. "Thank you, Maggie."

As Mom and Grandma opened their eyes, Priscilla hurried out the door, closing it behind her. She knew if anyone saw her, there would be trouble.

Out in the hallway, she thought about the book. *Why would her grandmother give her such a dangerous thing?* she wondered as she once again put her ear to the door.

She could hear her mother's faint voice. "What happened? Where's the book? I was just holding it."

"There it is," replied Grandma in an even weaker voice.

"The last thing I remember was opening the book, and then. . . "

Priscilla strained to hear what was being said inside the room. For a moment there was silence, and then Grandma spoke. "Don't be alarmed Frances. I think the magic has already started, and we got in the way."

"What do you mean?"

Again the conversation stopped, but Priscilla could hear someone moving towards the door.

"Look at the trail of dust on the floor," Grandma said finally. "It means that the book has made magic on its own. I'm sure of it."

"What can we do?"

"There is nothing for us to do now. The girls are the only ones who can control the book and its magic."

"Well then, let's wrap it quickly and be done with it," Mom replied, her voice trembling.

Again, Priscilla could hear stirring in the room. "And don't forget—leave it on the front porch tomorrow. I really want the girls to find it when they get home from school."

"Are you sure you don't want to give it to them yourself?"

"I'm sure. The girls don't need me looking over their shoulders when they open the book."

Satisfied she had heard enough and not wanting to be caught in the hallway, Priscilla hurried to the fireplace room. On the way, she took notice of the shimmering gray dust covering the floor. With each step she took, she watched the sparkling dust melt into the floor.

Nothing makes sense anymore . . . losing my mind? Maybe Penelope was right—maybe there is something wrong with me, she thought as she entered the room and walked over to the window.

Leaning her head against the glass, she gazed out into the yard. The moon was round and shone brightly through the trees. She watched as tall shadows swayed in the grass. Once again, she thought about the shimmering cloud. *I wonder what happened to it.*

"Things around here keep getting stranger and stranger," she said to herself as she noticed Mrs. Maven's cat, Pumpkin. He was sitting on the stone wall just below the window.

Rarely visible during the day, he seemed to prefer the night. Under the cover of darkness, he could tip over trashcans and trample gardens without being seen. But tonight, he showed no signs of having committed trouble of any kind. He looked content sitting and staring up at the window. *What was he doing? It looks as if he's looking right at me.*

Even from far away, Priscilla could see right into his eyes. They were dark and cold just like his owner's eyes. Goose bumps formed on her arms and she looked away. She quickly decided that she did not want him in her yard. She pushed open the window and called out to him. **"Go—get off our wall. Run . . . scat you mangy cat. Didn't your owner teach you any manners?"**

Pumpkin did not move or make a sound—he continued to watch Priscilla.

"Of course she didn't. She's too busy being crazy and harassing innocent people to take care of her pet," she said as she headed to her bedroom where she grabbed her robe, put on her sneakers, and headed downstairs. She heard her mother and grandmother go downstairs earlier, and she heard her mother come back upstairs and close her bedroom door, so she wasn't concerned about being caught.

Like a prowling animal, she quietly crept down the stairs, anger consuming every part of her. *How could they impose on her life that way?* She had to put a stop to it.

Downstairs, the moon had forgotten to lend its light to the rooms of the first floor. In the dark, she clumsily felt her way into the kitchen. A moment later, armed with a small pink teddy bear flashlight and a chocolate chip cookie, she waved the bear out in front of her and quickly made her way through the kitchen and laundry room, and then out into the backyard.

The air was bitterly cold, and the wind stung her face. Crunching her way in the frozen snow towards the stone wall, she noticed that the yard looked different—wild and overgrown. *That's odd—the yard didn't look this bad yesterday.*

Shining her flashlight over the wall, she was glad to see that Pumpkin was gone. *It's a good thing for him that he decided to leave.*

As she turned to head back to the house, something caught her eye—it was her house in the moonlight. Like the yard, it too looked different. When she shined the flashlight over the house, she almost fell backwards. "**What happened to our beautiful house?**"

The striking blue and white paint, the proud roof, and the beautiful stained glass windows were all gone. Once again, she shined her light over the yard. It was all gone—the house had returned to its previous condition. As she ran back to the house she wondered: *But, how did it happen?*

She had to talk to Maggie. She had to know if her friend had anything to do with what had happened.

Once in her room, she angrily summoned her friend. "Maggie . . . I need to talk to you," she cried. "Something has happened to our house . . . something terrible. I need to know if you had anything to do with it."

The wind began to howl, as did the walls of Priscilla's room. "I'm sorry, my friend," Maggie wailed.

Priscilla waited for more, but the walls were still.

"Is that it?" she asked angrily. "I know that you are upset about Penelope and me, but you didn't have to change yourself back. When the neighbors see the house, they will hate us again. You should have come to me first . . . that's what friends do," she cried, pacing around the room. "Say something. Say anything that will help me to understand why you have done such a thing."

Maggie spoke again, this time in a whisper louder than the times before, "Change is coming. Trust the magic. The magic is the key."

"I don't understand! You talk about trust . . . how can I trust you now? I just want you to restore yourself again," Priscilla wailed as she dropped down on her bed.

Looking around at the walls, she noticed that they were no longer illuminated, but looked cold and icy. It was proof that Maggie's pain not only showed on the surface, but went all the way to her core. Priscilla started to feel cold, too, and she knew that it was only a matter of time before the cold reached *her* core.

In a panic, she ran out of her room and down the dark hallway. *Mom will know what to do,* she thought; but then she stopped. *But, what if she doesn't believe me?*

A voice from within urged her to keep walking, and so she did. Halfway to her mother's room, she tripped, "Darn it Penelope! You shouldn't leave your shoes in the hallway."

Suddenly, Priscilla felt that she was not alone.

"Pardon me young lady, but I am *not* a shoe," said a tiny voice.

Priscilla looked around, but could see no one. As she searched for the hallway light switch she called out, "Who's there? Is that you Penelope? Stop playing games!"

When she finally turned the light on, she couldn't believe her eyes.

"So we meet again," said a large brown rat sitting on the carpet in front of her.

Priscilla covered her mouth with her trembling hands and muffled a scream.

The rat was sitting on its hind legs, looking up at her with sparkling black eyes.

"Get. . . Shoo . . . Scat!" she said as she kicked at the air. But the rat did not flinch.

Priscilla slowly backed down the hallway towards her room. She was afraid that if she turned her back on the creature, it would run after her and bite her heels.

"Don't be afraid. Maggie has sent me to you," called the rat in his squeaky little voice.

Priscilla felt her feet stop. "What am I doing? Rats can't talk."

Her mind started to race. Then, she thought about Maggie. *Well—if it is possible for a house to whisper then maybe a talking rat is not so impossible*, she decided.

Slowly, and with some hesitation, she turned around. "Who are you?" she timidly asked.

"My name is Oswald. And, as I have said, we met before."

Slowly, Priscilla moved closer to him. "I remember! You were the one that my sister and I saw when we moved here. But, how can you talk? Did Maggie give you this power?" she inquired, still trembling.

"It was not Maggie," he replied, smiling. It was the book—the book has made many things happen."

"Do you mean the book that my grandmother and mother had?"

"Yes . . . the magic has arrived, and there is more to come. But before I tell you any more, I must show you something."

Oswald turned away from Priscilla, exposing his back to her.

"What happened to your tail?" she gasped.

"The magic that the book creates is impure. When it acts alone, there are always consequences," Oswald replied, pointing to his stub.

"I'm not sure that I understand," said Priscilla, feeling more confused.

"Soon, everything will be clear, and my friends and I will help you along the way. Take me to your room and I'll tell you more."

Priscilla hesitated. In a million years, she never thought that she would be taking a rat back to her room, but this rat had kind and gentle eyes that let her know there was nothing to fear.

Once inside her room, Oswald took hold of Priscilla's blue and gray checked comforter and pulled himself up onto her bed. He puffed up his little chest and called out, "It is time my friends. Come out and welcome our newest friend."

Priscilla sat down on the bed and looked around. She had no idea what was going to happen, but felt open to just about anything at this point. A moment later, the bedroom door opened a crack, and an army of tiny fireflies flew into the room. They emerged, one-by-one, glowing softly and dancing above her head.

If this sort of thing had happened even a day earlier, she would have fainted. Now, she welcomed the glowing creatures.

"They're amazing! But why do they glow with a green light? I've never seen fireflies like that before."

"Another consequence of the book's magic. They, too, can speak, and they have come to welcome you to our house."

"*Your* house?"

"Yes. We have lived here for years, serving as companions to Maggie."

"We also help keep watch over her; and in return, she provides us with a home," said a soft-spoken firefly, as it flashed its green light. "Maggie has been waiting so long for a family to love her again."

"My name is Willow," said a smaller firefly, as she nudged her way past the others. "Maggie has a message for you. She wants you to know that she cannot always control her power. She is sorry for what has happened here tonight, and she has summoned the power of the book to help you."

Priscilla wondered why Maggie didn't give her this message herself.

"Thank you all for coming and bringing Maggie's message. It's good to know that I'm not alone," she said as her new friends disappeared out the door.

No longer feeling the urgency to tell her mother about the house, she went to bed.

During the night, a tapping sound on her bedroom door awakened her. "Who's there?" she whispered.

"Oswald," said the rat. "You need to see something."

"Can't it wait until tomorrow?" Priscilla asked sleepily.

"Well, no—it can't."

"Oh, all right. I'm coming," Priscilla said as she got out of bed, and once again put on her robe and sneakers. "It better be important."

Oswald and the fireflies were waiting out in the hallway.

"Well, let's go," Priscilla said.

The tiniest firefly, Willow, led the way through the dark hallway with her brilliant green glowing light. Along the way, Priscilla noticed that the shimmering gray dust had returned and she wondered: *Where could the cloud be?*

Down the stairs and out the back door, she hurried. She was curious to see where the path of the shimmering gray dust would end. Outside, the yard and the house were covered in a thin layer of the same dust. "What is going on here?" she asked, as she slowly made her way through the shimmering snow.

The air was still and the sky dark. The moonlight that fell softly upon the ground earlier that evening was now gone. But Priscilla could see well, for the shimmering dust was reflecting the green light from all of the fireflies.

"Is this what you wanted me to see?"

All of a sudden, an enormous gust of wind, with the strength of a tornado, began to whip around the yard. Priscilla fell to the ground and covered her head. A few seconds later, it was gone.

"What was that?" she asked, as she stood up and brushed off her robe.

Looking around, she saw that the shimmering dust was gone and the house and grounds had been restored. "**Oh, my goodness!**" she shouted, a huge smile emerging. "But how . . ."

Then Priscilla remembered that the firefly told her that Maggie was going to summon the power of the book.

"Maggie did what she promised," she exclaimed. "She summoned the power of the book to help me."

A second later, her face went pale. She remembered what Oswald said about the book's magic being impure. Walking around the outside of the house, she was thrilled to find everything intact.

"It's perfect! Oswald must have been mistaken."

Back inside the house, Priscilla turned on every light on the first floor. She was making sure that everything had been restored. "And to think, our house has been ruined and then restored all in one night. I can't believe that Mom and Penelope slept right through it," she said to herself, as she made her way into the parlor. "I won't dare tell them."

She glanced over at the clock on the mantle. It read one o'clock. Priscilla did not realize that it was so late. A moment later, a huge grin formed on her face.

"Hey—it's my birthday!" she said aloud.

Looking around the room, and smiling, she sat down on the sofa and spoke to Maggie. "Thank you so much for giving me the best birthday present ever."

Chapter Ten

Penelope Realizes the Truth

On the morning of their 13th birthday, Penelope and Priscilla sat at the kitchen table together, but did not speak.

"Would you girls please take a break from being mad at each other? It's your birthday for goodness sake," said Mom. "And, if you can't do it for my sake, do it for Grandma's—she's really looking forward to our visit later. I know for a fact that she baked you a special cake."

Penelope glanced over at her sister, who appeared to be engrossed in a book. "Maybe Mom's right, Priscilla. Let's put our differences aside for today. Okay?"

Priscilla looked up from her book and then over at her mother. "I guess I could do that for Mom's sake."

"That's great," Mom said, turning on the water. "Now, you girls should really be getting ready for school. You don't want to be late."

"We're going," Penelope said, taking one more bite of her toast.

Priscilla nodded her head in agreement, and the girls left the kitchen and went upstairs to get ready for school.

Outside, another bitterly cold February morning greeted them. Penelope was the first one out the door. Anxious to get to school, she wanted to see how her friends planned to celebrate her birthday. She had been talking about it for weeks and expected they would do something special for her. *Maybe they'll arrange for an announcement to be made after the homeroom bell.*

A moment later, Priscilla hurried down the steps.

"What took you so long?"

"I couldn't find one of my boots."

"Well, if you cleaned your room once in a while, maybe you would be able to find your stuff."

"Remember . . . we're supposed to be having a truce for today," Priscilla reminded her sister.

Penelope apologized, and the two started on their way. Once they had crossed the street, Mrs. Maven called to them from her porch. "Hey, girls! I would like for you both to come here for a minute," she said in an unusually kind voice.

"Ignore her—she's crazy," Priscilla said, and kept walking.

"Oh, come on . . . let's see what she wants," Penelope said, pulling her sister by the arm.

"Don't you remember what she did to me in the woods?"

"It's two against one," Penelope said, grinning, as she tried to persuade her sister to go.

"Okay, I'll go with you, but just for a minute," Priscilla said finally.

As the girls walked slowly up the icy porch steps, Penelope noticed that Mrs. Maven had disappeared, but she had left her front door open, allowing an odd smell to waft through the screen door.

"What *is* that smell?" whispered Penelope, wrinkling her nose.

"Oh, don't worry," said Mrs. Maven as she popped her head out the door. "That's just breakfast for Pumpkin. I don't feed him just any food—I prepare it myself. He deserves only the best."

Penelope hated Pumpkin, even more than Priscilla did. Last summer, he not only attacked her, but he also dug up her petunias, ate her begonias, and left dead mice on their front lawn.

"He sure is lucky to have you," she said, trying to smile.

"Well, we'd love to chat some more, but we're going to be late for school," Priscilla said as she jerked her sister towards the stairs.

As Penelope plunged forward, her backpack slid off her shoulder.

"**Wait a minute, Priscilla!**" she shouted and stopped at the porch's edge.

Penelope glanced over her shoulder at Mrs. Maven, who was standing in the doorway. Bending down quickly, she reached for her backpack. As she grabbed the shoulder strap, Priscilla shouted, "**Behind you, Penelope!**"

Penelope looked up just as Mrs. Maven grabbed her arm. The backpack fell to the floor.

"**Let me go!**"

"You can't leave yet. There is something that I want you to see," Mrs. Maven said in a sinister tone, letting go of Penelope's arm.

Priscilla ran up onto the porch and grabbed her sister. "Come on. Let's get out of here!"

As the two ran down the steps, Mrs. Maven shouted, **"Look!"**

"Wait!" Penelope cried when she realized that the old woman was pointing to their house.

The two stopped and Priscilla let out a loud sigh. **"Why can't you just leave us alone?"**

Mrs. Maven laughed. "You probably thought that no one would find out," she said, her mouth glistening with drool.

Penelope noticed how pleased Mrs. Maven was with herself. *What is she up to?*

"Find out *what?*" asked Priscilla.

"Find out that your house is not what it appears to be. I know that you witches have cast some sort of spell on the house. But you made a mistake. There is a place just below the parlor window where I can see the chipped and weathered wood," she announced, proudly. "Come and see for yourself. Your house has a *tear!*"

The old woman motioned for the girls to come and take a look. But before Penelope could say a word, or move a muscle, Priscilla pulled her down the walkway. "We really have to go, right Penelope?" she said.

"Yeah, we're going to be late for school," Penelope replied, following her sister.

As the girls headed back towards Second Street, they could hear Mrs. Maven yelling after them. **"I'm not through with you two. I'm not going to stop until I expose all of you for what you really are. Then, I will be respected and you will be the outcasts."**

When they reached Second Street, Penelope realized that she didn't have her backpack. "**Darn!** With everything that happened back there, I never got my backpack. You go ahead, and I'll catch up," she said.

"Wait! I don't want you to go back there alone. I'll go too."

"No! We can't both be late. If I'm not back before the chimes sound, tell Jasmine to wait on the birthday announcement till I get there."

Priscilla reluctantly agreed, but ignored her sister's delusional request about delaying the announcement.

"Before I go, there's something that you should know," said Priscilla. "I didn't tell you this earlier because we weren't talking, but after what Mrs. Maven said, I have to tell you."

Penelope crossed her arms in front of her. "Okay, tell me."

"Last night some really strange things happened to our house. First, Maggie, our house, turned herself back to the crumbling mess she was when we moved in. Then she sent a rat named Oswald and an army of fireflies to deliver a message to me. They told me that Maggie would send the magic of the book to restore her. Oswald also told me that the book's magic is always flawed. That would explain the tear. I searched the house inside and out, but I guess I missed it."

"Slow down—I don't understand! Your story about the whispering walls was bad enough, but talking rats and magical books. I know that I told Mom that I would keep an open mind, but this is too much."

Penelope paused and rubbed the back of her neck. "Priscilla—I'm really worried about you. Our house is fine. Just look at it . . . nothing has changed," she said, pointing to their house.

"Well, maybe the book cast some sort of cloaking spell on the house to hide the old exterior. What we really need to do, is to go up on her porch and see this tear for ourselves," Priscilla replied.

"Not that I believe any of this, but what is this magical book that you keep ranting about?"

"It's our birthday present from Grandma. I overheard Mom and Grandma talking in Mom's room last night."

Penelope glanced down at her watch. "Can we talk about this later? I really have got to get my backpack. It has my diary and letters to my new boyfriend, Gary, in it. We'll talk later . . . I promise," she said as she turned around and hurried down the sidewalk.

As she approached Mrs. Maven's porch, Penelope noticed that the front door was still open. She hoped she wouldn't be discovered as she crept up the stairs and over to where she had dropped her backpack. As she bent down to grab it, she thought about what her sister had said earlier. *Why does Priscilla make up these fantastic lies?*

As she started back down the steps, she heard voices coming from the house. *Who would Mrs. Maven be talking to? I didn't think she had any friends.*

Even though she knew she'd be really late to school, she had to know who else was there. In hopes that no one would see her, she turned and crouched down outside the door and listened.

"One minute I was chasing a mouse in their yard, meowing like I always do, and the next minute I was talking to that rat. I told him that I was going to catch him and eat him for breakfast. But, then I realized that I had no teeth. From now on, you'll have to mash up all of my food," said a raspy voice.

"I'm sorry to hear about your teeth, but I am upset to think that you prefer mice to my food," whined Mrs. Maven.

"Well, now that I can talk . . . I have to tell you something. I'm sorry, but I hate boiled eel and squash"

Penelope could not believe her ears. *What's happening to me? First I'm spying on people, and now I'm hearing things.*

She had to know if her suspicions were right.

Crawling over to the window, she peered through the sheer dingy white curtains. Her ears had not played tricks on her. She could clearly see Mrs. Maven and Pumpkin sitting on the sofa in the living room, engaged in conversation. She observed Pumpkin's mouth as it moved. She noticed that he was, indeed, toothless.

"Priscilla's been telling me the truth all along," she said to herself, trembling with fear. "I guess I needed to see it for myself."

Once Penelope pulled herself together, she crawled back over to the front door and continued to listen.

"I can spy on them for you, too. I spend a lot of time in their yard anyway," said Pumpkin.

"Would you do that for me?" replied Mrs. Maven, her voice cracking.

"Why not? You take care of me; and besides, I know that they hate me."

Penelope wondered what Pumpkin meant by, "spy on them, too." *Is someone already spying on us?*

She listened for a couple more seconds and made mental notes of everything that she heard. As she was about to leave, she remembered the tear and wondered if that, too, was real. She looked at the spot under the parlor window that Mrs. Maven was ranting about.

"I can't believe it," she said to herself. "There it was, just like Mrs. Maven said—a large patch of faded and chipped blue siding. "Priscilla was right about this, too."

Later that day on the way home from school, Penelope told her sister everything that happened at Mrs. Maven's house.

"I'm glad to hear that you finally believe me," said Priscilla.

"I almost wish I didn't. What are we going to do about Mrs. Maven and Pumpkin? They think that we're witches."

Priscilla grinned. "You know . . . not all witches are bad?"

"What are you talking about?"

"When I told you about what happened last night, I left out the part when Mom referred to herself as a *great witch*."

Penelope looked pale. "You're kidding, right?"

"No, I'm not. And just think of what the townspeople will do to us if they find out."

"I don't want to think about any of it. We can't be witches," Penelope said, feeling a little queasy.

"I'm sorry Penelope, but everything that I told you is true and whether you like it or not, we have to do something to ensure that Mrs. Maven doesn't tell anyone."

Penelope began to sweat. "Priscilla, I'm starting to feel sick."

Priscilla put her arm around her sister. "Don't worry Penelope, we'll think of something. Remember what I said about the magic of the book? Well, maybe it can help us."

"I . . . I don't know Priscilla. I don't think that I can handle any of this."

"Yes you can. I'll help you."

"But, you don't understand . . . there's something I didn't tell you. I didn't want to talk about it before, but now I realize that I have to tell you the reason why I've been so opposed to magic."

Priscilla crossed her arms in front of her. "Please tell me. I would love to know," she said sarcastically.

"Don't say it like that. This is really hard for me," Penelope said as she kicked a pebble into the grass.

"I'm sorry. Tell me."

"Okay, here goes…"

"When we were seven, Mom took me to the mall one Saturday to buy a new dress. You didn't go because you and Dad wanted to watch some kind of basketball or baseball game on TV. Anyway, there was a magic show going on near the mall's food court. I couldn't believe how many people had stopped shopping to watch a guy named *Waldo the Great* separate colored rings and pull a squirrel out from an empty salad bowl—the usual boring magic stuff. I would never have stopped to watch the show, but I had already found my dress and I was hungry so Mom ordered me a corn dog. Well, just as Mom and I finished eating and were getting ready to leave, something really interesting finally happened."

"What?"

"The magician's assistant wheeled a huge glass box up onto the stage. She asked for a volunteer from the audience to get into the box. The only person to raise their hand was a chubby woman with frizzy bleached blonde hair and big, red-rimmed sunglasses. She seemed overly eager to participate—she actually ran onto the stage. After the woman lay down in the box, the magician locked it and covered it with his long silver cape. Then he said a few magic words."

Penelope stopped talking and stared at the sidewalk.

"What happened next?" Priscilla eagerly asked.

Penelope looked up at her sister and with tears in her eyes said, "She disappeared."

Priscilla rolled her eyes. "Well, isn't that what is supposed to happen in the *disappearing lady* trick?"

"No . . . you don't get it! I mean, she really disappeared! After the magician said the words to bring her back, nothing happened. Mom tried to tell me that it was all part of the trick, but I knew better—I saw the commotion. First the mall security came, then the police, and then the newspaper reporters and TV crew."

Penelope was trembling as she spoke. "The woman was no where to be found, and I never forgot about her. I wondered where that horrible man had sent her. Was it to another dimension or somewhere worse?"

"Calm down Penelope. It's okay. That was a long time ago," Priscilla said as she put her arm around her sister.

"No, it wasn't . . . that's what I'm trying to tell you. All of this talk about magic has been bringing that day back to me. It's really about now. I'm scared, Priscilla," Penelope said as she wiped her eyes.

"Why didn't you tell me all of this before?" asked Priscilla.

"At first, I was too afraid to even talk about it. Then, over time, I guess I worried that you would think I was being a baby."

"What about Mom and Dad? Why didn't you tell them?"

Penelope paused. "I don't know, maybe I should have."

For the next couple of blocks, Priscilla was very quiet.

"Are you okay? Is something wrong?" Penelope asked her sister.

Priscilla stopped and dropped her backpack to the ground. "I've been thinking about the disappearing lady and I think I remember hearing something about her on the news."

"*Really?*"

"Yeah, but it wasn't about her disappearance, it was about her capture."

Penelope looked puzzled. "*Capture?* What are you talking about?"

"Now, I remember," Priscilla said, looking up at the sky. "About a month after the woman from the mall disappeared, the police found someone matching her description in another state. She had been arrested for attempting to rob a hot dog stand. From what I heard, the woman had a lot of financial problems and was looking for a way out. She was in the mall the day of the magic show to look for a new wig when she realized that she could use the disappearing trick to leave town. She figured that, eventually, people would stop looking for her and she could start a new life for herself somewhere else."

Penelope couldn't believe her ears. "Are you *sure* the police had the right woman?"

"That's what I heard."

"I can't believe it . . . she's *really* okay?"

"Yup—I'm sure she's safe and sound in some woman's prison."

Penelope let out a sigh. "For all these years, I've been afraid of magic for no reason."

"Does this mean that you'll give the book a chance?"

"I don't know, Priscilla. I think I need some time."

"I understand, but we don't have much time. The book is probably sitting on our porch as we speak."

"I guess you're right. Tell me what I need to know," Penelope said as she pushed her hair behind her ears

"I'll do my best," replied Priscilla.

From the edge of Nelson Woods to Second Street, Priscilla told her sister everything she knew about the book. After she was done, Penelope started to tell her about her day.

"It was so sweet—Jasmine and the gang sang me a special birthday song. And, after math, my friend Sandy gave me a pink teddy bear cake," she said, bubbling with happiness.

Priscilla smiled and nodded. "I'm happy for you, Penelope."

Moments later, when the girls approached their house, Priscilla nudged her sister and pointed. "Penelope, look! There's a big box on our front porch."

"Do you think it's the book?" Penelope asked as she hurried up the porch steps and tripped. "Ouch!" she said as she landed on the large cardboard box. "Ooooh, look! I got my dress dirty." She quickly got up and started wiping at the smudge.

"It's from Grandma. It's the book! I told you that it would be here," Priscilla announced, smiling. "Grab an end."

"Great—I can *hardly* wait to open it," Penelope said sarcastically as she lifted her end. "What are the odds that you misunderstood what you heard last night? Grandma could have said that she was giving us a radical book—like a magazine subscription to *Hot Fashions Monthly*.

With that, Priscilla gently lowered her end of the box. "Penelope, this is no time for jokes. Don't you get it? This book is important. Maggie says that the magic is the key and that we should trust it. I believe the magic she spoke of is in this book."

Penelope accidentally dropped her end and the box fell to the floor with a *slam*.

"What are you doing?" Priscilla wailed. "Be careful, you don't want to upset the book."

"I'm sorry. I didn't mean to do that. But, what did you mean by what you just said? What is the magic supposed to be the key to?"

"The key to everything—getting by in this town, bringing us closer, and stopping Mrs. Maven," Priscilla explained. "Maybe we can turn her into a toad or something."

Penelope was not amused. "I already told you that I'm still feeling a little spooked about all of this magic stuff. So, if there is a magical book in here, you'll have to deal with it."

"Fine, I'm sure that I can handle it on my own. Grab your end and let's go," Priscilla said as she lifted her end. "And, remember to act surprised—I don't want Mom to know that I was spying on her."

Penelope nodded and grabbed the other end of the box.

Once inside, the girls carefully placed the box on the floor.

"Mom, we're home. Come see what we found on the porch," Priscilla shouted.

Mom quickly came in from the kitchen and greeted the girls. "What do you have there?" she asked

"Grandma sent us something for our birthday. We're going to go upstairs and open it," replied Priscilla.

"Okay—let me know what she sent," Mom said with a grin.

The girls took hold of the box once more and headed up the stairs.

"Let's open it in the fireplace room," suggested Penelope.

Priscilla agreed, and the two of them carried their gift up the stairs. The girls placed the box down in the center of the room and sat on either side of it.

"Even though you've told me what our gift is, this is still kind of exciting," said Penelope. Then she had a thought and a huge smiled formed. "Priscilla—don't you think that the box is big enough to hold more than one present? I mean . . . maybe Grandma sent the book for you and, maybe . . . a new outfit for me."

"No matter what Grandma sent us, it's not going to do either of us any good if we don't take it out of the box."

"I guess you're right," said Penelope as she began to tear at the wrapping tape.

Priscilla grabbed the other end and together they popped open the cardboard flaps.

Bending over the open box, the girls pulled the tissue paper away and peered inside. Underneath the layers of paper they found a book that seemed to glisten and glow. It was so colorful and amazing that they were both delighted by it. The book was covered with brightly colored pieces of cloth cut in various shapes. There were no words on the cover, only glittery swirls and silver stars that shimmered, giving the book a magical appearance.

"**This is it! This is the book I saw in Mom's room!**" shouted Priscilla.

Together, the girls gently lifted the book from the box. Once out, Penelope let the book go and Priscilla placed it on her lap. She immediately opened it and shielded her head with her hand. When nothing happened, she smiled and read from the first page, *Recipes, Spells, and Secrets*.

"The title sure sounds mystical enough. I have a feeling that this book is connected to all of the strange things that have happened lately," Priscilla said as she carefully placed the book on the floor.

She began to rifle through the yellow tissue paper, searching for a card or a letter. "It would be helpful if

Grandma included a card or something, but I don't see one," she said.

Suddenly, the pages of the book started to turn by themselves and the girls moved closer together.

"What's happening, Priscilla?" Penelope asked as she grabbed her sister's arm.

"I don't know . . . but it's stopping."

Summoning up all her courage, Priscilla slowly lifted the book and read from the page that the book had opened up to: "*Transformation Spell.*"

"This is really creepy. How did it do that? Why do you think it stopped on that page?" whispered Penelope.

"Well, I overheard Mom and Grandma say that the book will show us what to do. Maybe it wants us to perform this *Transformation Spell.*"

Penelope started to whine, "I'm scared Priscilla. What are we going to do?"

The expression on Priscilla's face softened. "Calm down, Penelope. It's going to be okay. I don't think that we should be afraid of the book. It's here to help us."

Penelope was not sure she believed her sister. "Why are you always so sure about everything?" she asked.

Priscilla told her sister all about her conversation with Mom. "Are you saying that you and Mom have some sort of special powers?" asked Penelope.

"Not necessarily powers—it's more like strong hunches about things."

Penelope wondered if she had these feelings too.

"Why don't we wait and talk to Grandma tonight," said Priscilla. "I'm sure that she'll explain everything."

Penelope agreed to give the matter a rest. While she went to her room to lie down, Priscilla took the book to her room for safe-keeping.

Later that day, Penelope and Mom waited in the kitchen for Priscilla to come downstairs.

"So . . . you haven't said anything about your gift from Grandma. What did she give you?" Mom asked in her usual cheerful tone.

"Uh . . . well, it was something that I would have never expected. It's a book about recipes, spells, and something else," said Penelope, trying to remember. "Maybe you would know . . . why did Grandma give us such a book? Is it for real?"

"I think that Grandma wants to tell you about the book. Why don't you ask her about it tonight?"

"Do you think that it would be okay if we brought the book with us?"

Mom smiled. "I know that Grandma would want you to."

Less than ten minutes later, Mom's car approached Grandma's street. As Priscilla read the name, *Landing Lane*, she grabbed the book and sat up straight in the seat. It was six o'clock sharp when they pulled up in front of Grandma's small woodsy-green ranch-style house. Before getting out of the car, Penelope smoothed her hair and dress.

"I hope that Grandma made the same chocolate cake as last year," Priscilla said as the three walked up the brick path.

Penelope rang the bell and Grandma opened the door and greeted the girls with a warm smile. "Hello, girls—happy birthday!"

"Hi Grandma," Penelope replied, giving her grandmother a big hug.

Priscilla followed closely behind, holding the book in front of her.

"I see that you got my present. I'm glad that you brought it with you. As I said in my card, the book must not be left alone until you learn how to control its power," said Grandma.

Penelope and Priscilla looked at each other. "What card?" they asked.

Grandma's eyes squinted. "Good heavens! Did I forget to include the card?"

Both girls nodded.

"I'm so sorry. I do seem to forget things from time-to-time."

"That's okay, but we were a little confused," said Priscilla.

"I'm sure you were," replied Grandma as she led everyone into the living room.

After they sat down, Priscilla placed the book on the coffee table in front of her. "Now, I'm sure that you girls are anxious for me to tell you everything I know about the book," said Grandma.

"Yeah," replied Priscilla.

Penelope nodded. Grandma picked up the book and glanced in Mom's direction. "This book has a long and colorful history, dating back more than 200 years," she said as she ran her fingers over the cover. "It belonged to our ancestors, a group of people called, the Enlightened Ones."

"The Enlightened Ones?" interrupted Penelope. "You're kidding right?"

"No, I'm not," Grandma replied, very seriously. "May I continue?"

Penelope blushed and gave a small nod.

"The Enlightened Ones were a sect or group of people who had special abilities. The head of the Enlightened

Ones was a man named Abisius. He had abilities and knowledge surpassing those of anyone in the sect. During his first year as leader, he wrote this book," Grandma explained. "Filled with magical recipes, secrets, and spells, the book was intended to be a guide for our people. Abisius hoped that the book's power would help to bring peace and happiness to all members of society. As it turned out, he was the only one who could make magic with the book. But, over time, even his powers weakened. He realized that it was necessary to make the book's magic accessible to all members of the sect, but this was an immense responsibility—even for such a powerful person as Abisius."

Grandma paused and put down the book. "What happened to Abisius?" Penelope asked.

"In time, he found a way to grant the power of the book to others," replied Grandma. "He chose a member of the sect whom he trusted and whom he felt possessed exceptional natural abilities. This is how my great-great-great grandfather took possession of the book—I understand he was a very special man."

Penelope felt her stomach churn.

"When I turned 16, my grandmother, who had possession of the book, felt that I was ready to receive it. I, in turn, gave it to your mother on her 16th birthday," continued Grandma.

"Now, you've given it to us," said Priscilla.

Grandma nodded. "Hey, wait a minute," said Penelope. "Does this mean that we have special powers too?

Grandma and Mom looked at each other.

"Your grandmother and I knew from the minute you were born that you were both very special. Since Priscilla has shown signs of having special abilities, it's only a matter of time until you show them too," replied Mom.

Penelope stood up and put her hands on her hips. "What special abilities has Priscilla shown?"

"Priscilla is sensitive to the natural forces—that's why Maggie has come to her," said Mom. "Priscilla has an open mind—that's the first thing a truly gifted Enlightened One needs to have."

"Are you trying to say that I'm *not* special because I *don't* have an open mind?" Penelope asked, sitting down next to her mother.

Mom moved closer to her. "What you need to do is try to be a little more willing to believe in things that don't seem logically possible."

"Like magic?" asked Penelope.

"That's right," Mom replied, smiling.

Penelope paused for a moment. "Okay, I'll try," she finally said.

Priscilla stood up and walked over to Grandma. "Now, if you two are finished, I'd like to ask Grandma something."

"What is it dear?"

"Why did you give us the book now? We're only 13."

Grandma took a deep breath. "Because your mother and I thought that the two of you could use it now."

"I'm not sure that I understand," Priscilla said, sitting down on the loveseat next to her grandmother.

"Your mother and I have watched the two of you drift apart. We feel that it is time for you to find each other again. The book will help you do that. Now . . . please let me finish my story."

"Okay."

"Since the book is very powerful, it has the ability to do magic on its own. But this magic is impure, and will always have negative consequences."

"That's what Oswald told me," said Priscilla.

"Who's Oswald?" inquired Mom, giving her daughter a suspicious look.

"Uh—it's a long story," replied Priscilla. "I'll tell you everything later."

Grandma looked annoyed. "If you two are done, I'd like to continue."

Mom and Priscilla smiled at each other.

"That is why the book must be controlled. Left alone, it can be dangerous," said Grandma, in a serious tone.

Penelope leaned across the coffee table and grabbed the book. "As I said, Penelope—the book is very powerful. You must watch how you handle it or . . . "Grandma warned.

"Or *what*?" What could this book do to me?"

A second later, Penelope let out a scream and dropped the book to the floor with a loud *thump*.

"It burned me! That book really burned me," she shouted, holding her hand.

"Let me see," said Mom inspecting Penelope's hand. "There's nothing there. The book was just deceiving you."

Mom was right. There was no mark on Penelope's hand.

"That was the book's way of telling you that it means business," said Grandma, gently picking up the book. "You must treat it with great respect."

"All right—I get it," said Penelope, feeling embarrassed.

Grandma continued. "You must both work together—the magic you make will be impure unless you work together. That means listening to each other and trusting each other. You must also learn to follow your instincts—they will never steer you wrong. And, lastly, you must believe in the book's power. Only then will you have access to the book's magic."

"But why does the book need both of us?" whined Penelope. "Priscilla is the one who likes all of this magic stuff."

"The forces of nature brought you both into this world together, so together you must work to bring about the magic," explained Mom. "You are twin sisters—you have a connection, even if you don't want to see it now. If you work together with the book, you will make powerful magic."

"I would prefer not to make any magic—it frightens me," replied Penelope.

"Yeah, it seems that Penelope's fear of magic started when we were seven. Just today she finally explained the reason why she's been anti-magic," Priscilla said as she stood up.

Mom and Grandma looked at Penelope.

"What happened?" Mom asked.

Penelope repeated her story about the disappearing woman.

"As I recall, that woman was found living in another state. She had assumed a new identity and everything," Mom said.

"I told you so," said Priscilla.

Penelope was a little embarrassed. "And that's why you have to give me a little time to warm up to all of this."

Mom put her arm around her daughter. I just want you to know that when Grandma gave me the book, I was scared, too. But, as soon as I learned how to perform some spells, I realized that making magic was more fun than it was scary," she explained. "Now that you know the truth about that woman's disappearance, I hope you'll give magic a chance."

Listening to Mom talk, Penelope realized how important it was for her to try. "Okay, Mom, I'll do my best."

"Thank you," said Mom as she hugged her daughter.

Turning to look at her sister, Penelope noticed that she had a far off look on her face. "Earth to Priscilla," she called.

Priscilla quickly came around. "What's wrong?" she asked. "Why is everyone staring at me?"

"Is anything wrong, Priscilla? You seem troubled," Grandma inquired.

Priscilla was quiet for a moment. "Well, I have a couple of questions," she replied.

"Of course dear, what would you like to know?"

Priscilla's expression was very serious. "I found a doll in the attic. It belonged to the little girl who used to live in our house. I was told that the doll is pretty special. I was wondering if it might be magical. Is there anything about a magical doll in the book?"

Grandma took off her glasses and rubbed her eyes. "It has been a long time since I've read from the book, but I do not recall reading about a special doll. Please bring it with you the next time you come, I'd like to take a look at it."

"Okay."

"Was there anything else?"

"Oh, yeah . . . I was wondering what happened to the Enlightened Ones? Are we the only ones left?"

Mom and Grandma looked at each other. "I'm sure that there are some others," replied Grandma.

Once again, Priscilla joined her grandmother on the loveseat.

"There's something that I need to tell you girls," Mom announced suddenly.

"What?" Penelope asked.

"Well, Dunville was the original home of our people. Grandma told me this when she gave me the book. That's why we moved here."

Penelope and Priscilla gasped.

"Wow!" said Priscilla, as she stood up and walked over to the picture window. "Did they live among the other townspeople?"

"Yes," said Grandma. "Very peacefully, until the day a member of the sect stole the book. Her intention was to use the magic of the book to take over the town. In the end, she was unsuccessful and the book was returned to its master. Unfortunately, the townspeople found out about her plans and were furious. Little-by-little, they drove our people away."

"I have the feeling that some of our people returned to Dunville when they thought it was safe," Mom added.

Penelope became frightened. "Mom, are we safe living in Dunville?" she asked.

"Of course," Mom replied, grabbing Penelope's hand. "No one knows about us or the book."

Priscilla continued to stare out the window. "I'm not so sure about that," she muttered and turned to her mother. "Remember what our neighbor said about the people who threatened their way of life?"

"Yes."

"Do you think they were talking about the Enlightened Ones?"

"Unfortunately, I do."

Penelope stood up. "What will happen to us if the townspeople find out about us?" she said.

Grandma stood up, too. "That's where you two come in. Together with the book, you have the power to do great things—even protect our kind," she said as she put her arm around Penelope.

"Hey Penelope, can I talk to you for a minute?" Priscilla called from across the room.

"What's wrong?" asked Penelope, as she joined her sister.

"We have to tell Mom about Mrs. Maven's threats."

Penelope agreed and together they told Mom and Grandma everything about Mrs. Maven and what happened on her porch earlier that day.

"Mom, she called us witches. Is she right?" Penelope asked. "Are we witches?"

Mom and Grandma looked at each other.

"Do you want to handle this one?" Mom said to Grandma.

Grandma picked up the book. "Yes, Penelope, we are.
Witchcraft is the foundation of this book. The fact that Mrs. Maven referred to us as witches is truly disturbing."

"But, how could she know?" asked Priscilla.

"I don't know," Mom said as she ran her fingers through her hair. "I can't believe that I didn't see it coming. You told me about Mrs. Maven, but I didn't want to believe that it would go this far. What are we going to do? You're not ready."

"Let's not panic," said Grandma. "They will just have to learn quickly."

"We can do it, I know that we can," Priscilla said as she put her arm around her sister. "We have the book—that may just be enough. From now on, we have to listen to each other and stick together if we're going to survive in this town."

Everyone stared at Priscilla. "Boy, you sure have taken a turn," said Mom.

"Yeah, Priscilla—since when did *you* become the leader?" asked Penelope.

Priscilla straightened herself and stood tall. "I'm not sure, but I think it's the magic."

"And don't forget, I'll be there to help you both for as long as you need me," Mom said, smiling.

Later that evening in Grandma's kitchen, Penelope pulled Priscilla aside. "What did you mean by 'we have the book—that may just be enough?'" she asked. "Are you saying that we should use some kind of spell to stop Mrs. Maven?"

"Well—I guess I am. We have to do *something*."

Penelope looked like she was about to cry. "Maybe Mrs. Maven will forget about the tear, and we can go on with our lives."

"Boy Penelope! I really thought that you were beginning to understand what's going on here. I can't believe that you would even suggest that Mrs. Maven would simply forget about the tear and all of her crazy suspicions. She has nothing to do but sit on her porch, looking to find someone to pay for her misery and loneliness."

Penelope's head felt like it was going to explode. It had been a long day, and she was tired of talking about magic. "Why don't we talk about all of this tomorrow? I heard Mom say that she wanted to go home," she muttered as she searched for her coat.

With their coats on, the girls sat in silence while Mom said goodbye to Grandma.

On the way home, the mood inside the car was hushed. Penelope looked over at her sister, who was slumped down in her seat, clenching the book tightly, and looking out the window. *I know that I agreed we should stick together, and I'll try to do my part; but, I have a life—and commitments. I'm not like Priscilla—I just can't put my life on hold because that book came into our lives.*

When they arrived home, Penelope decided not to think about the book anymore. Jasmine was coming over the next day and she needed to pick out her clothes.

Chapter Eleven

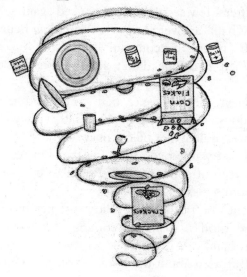

Priscilla Forgets Her Grandmother's Warning

On Saturday, Priscilla awoke and pulled on her blue bathrobe, and after grabbing the book, she went downstairs for breakfast. *I can't wait to read the book,* she thought to herself. *I hope Penelope will be down soon.*

As she gently placed the book on the kitchen table, she wondered how she would know when the book was safe to leave alone. Grandma had forgotten to tell them that part, and toting around the heavy book was becoming a nuisance.

After breakfast, she went upstairs to wake Penelope. *"Knock, knock,"* she gently tapped on her door. There was no answer.

After a few seconds, she knocked again.

"What?" answered a groggy sounding Penelope.

"It's me. Can I come in?"

When Penelope didn't answer, Priscilla opened the door.

"Hey! I didn't say that you could come in. If someone doesn't answer, that means that they're sleeping," Penelope said, pulling her pillow over her head.

"I just wanted you to know that I'm ready whenever you are to try out some magic," Priscilla said as she stepped into the room.

Penelope pushed the pillow off her head and rolled over. "I can't today. Jasmine's coming over later. She's going to color my hair."

"But what about the book? You agreed to work with me. You know that I can't do it alone."

"Can't it wait till tomorrow? I don't have any plans for tomorrow."

Priscilla was disappointed. "What choice do I have," she said as she left the room.

Two hours later, Priscilla sat in the parlor studying when the doorbell rang. "Just a minute," she called as she dragged herself from the sofa and headed into the foyer. Opening the door, she found Jasmine standing there, holding a sparkly purple bag overflowing with clips, combs, brushes, a hairdryer, and several colored bottles. "Hi, Jasmine—I'll get Penelope," she said, leaving Jasmine standing in the doorway.

"What kind of book is that?" Jasmine asked suddenly, smacking her gum. "It looks kind of old."

"It was a birthday present from my grandmother. It's a very special book for Penelope and me," Priscilla replied, cradling the book in her arms.

Jasmine looked unimpressed.

"Hi, Jasmine! How's it going?" Penelope asked as she bounded down the stairs a moment later.

"I'm great! Are you ready to get started?"

"Yeah! Why don't we go to the upstairs bathroom?"

"That's a great idea—I'll come too," Priscilla said, starting up the stairs with the book.

When no one followed, Priscilla felt embarrassed.

"Hello, Jasmine. What are you two up to today?" Mom asked as she came in from the kitchen.

Penelope told her mother about her plans.

"If you must do this, then why don't you use the kitchen sink. You'll have more room," Mom suggested.

Suddenly feeling like a third wheel, Priscilla decided that watching her sister have her hair colored did not seem very exciting, so she went to her room instead. Once inside, she shut the door, laid the book on her bed, and plopped down next to it. Staring up at the ceiling, she began to feel sorry for herself. "Maggie, I don't know what I'm going to do. I don't seem to fit into Penelope's world anymore. And I hate feeling jealous of Jasmine. I know that I have my own friends now, but I still feel like something is missing—like a part of me is missing."

Maggie revealed herself to Priscilla in her usual manner, except this time the wind did not howl—it hummed sadly. "I will help where I can . . . but you must have faith. You must have faith that the ones you love will be there when it really counts," she whispered.

Priscilla could feel Maggie's sadness. *If it were water,* she thought, *it would be leaking from every crack and crevasse in her room, filling it, and lifting her up to the ceiling.*

"There have been a lot of times recently when I really needed Penelope, and she wasn't there for me. I had faith in her, but she blew it," she said angrily.

"Do not worry. Change is coming," Maggie whispered.

Now, the wind began to howl, shaking the walls and rattling the windows. Priscilla felt glad that she had Maggie to talk to, even though she didn't always understand her.

Feeling a little bit better, Priscilla decided to go back downstairs. She wanted to be there in case Jasmine messed up her sister's hair.

Approaching the kitchen, she heard Penelope's voice. "Are you sure that you've done this before, Jasmine?"

"Of course—dozens of times."

Priscilla entered the kitchen and saw her sister bent over the kitchen sink, a fluffy orange towel draped over her shoulders to protect her clothing. Jasmine stood over her, pouring a gloppy purple solution on her hair.

"What's that you're pouring? It sort of tingles," Penelope said as Jasmine continued to pour the liquid.

"It's the highlighting solution. You said that you wanted to have some subtle highlights."

"Uh . . . of course. I did say that, didn't I?"

After Jasmine finished rinsing the highlighting solution from Penelope's hair, she wrapped her head in a yellow and white striped towel. As Penelope blotted her hair with the towel, the lights in the kitchen started to flicker, and the air grew cool.

"What's going on?" Penelope asked as she stood up. As she stomped towards the foyer she called, "Mom—where are you? There's something wrong with the lights."

A moment later, Mom rushed into the kitchen. "What's wrong?" she asked. *"Brrrrr!* It's cold in here. Did someone go outside and leave the back door open?" she asked, rubbing her arms. "The draft in here is terrible."

The girls looked at each other. "It wasn't me," all three answered in unison.

"Mom, did you notice the lights flickering?" asked Priscilla.

"No, they were fine in the den. Let me go into the basement and take a look."

"Will *someone* close that back door!" Penelope shouted.

"Calm down—I'll go," Priscilla offered. As she walked toward the back door, the draft intensified and the wind outside began to howl. "Is that you, Maggie?" she whispered.

Maggie did not respond.

The air in the kitchen had grown unbearably cold. When Priscilla reached the door, she saw that it was closed and locked, and she also noticed that there was no longer a draft. "What's going on around here?" she asked herself as she glanced out the window.

She gasped when she saw Sarah's doll lying outside in the snow. She unlocked the door immediately and flung it open. As she did so, an immense gust of wind whipped up, knocking her back against the door. With a throbbing ache in both her neck and lower back, she tried to stand. When she was finally able to get to her feet, she looked around and wondered: *Where did that come from?*

Stepping out into the cold glistening snow, she wondered why these bizarre things were happening. Then, she thought about the book and quickly realized that she had left it alone. "The book," she said out loud. "I left it in my room. How could I be so forgetful?"

147

Worried that her mother would discover that she had left the enchanted book alone, she quickly ran through the snow, grabbed the doll, and ran back to the house.

Back in the kitchen, she was greeted with a scene that made her question her sanity.

All of the kitchen cabinets were wide open, and their contents were sailing around in the air like miniature kites caught in a cyclone.

Shocked, she stood in the doorway and watched as dishes and glasses, as well as canned and boxed foods collided with each other and then fell to the floor before her. Her impulse was to run away, but a voice inside her told her that she must stay. She wondered: *Where's Penelope?*

It only took a moment for Priscilla to spot her sister and Jasmine huddled under the kitchen table. **"Are you guys okay?"** she yelled.

Priscilla could see her sister's lips move, but could not hear her response. The clattering noise had intensified. Overhead, she watched as her mother's favorite sugar bowl soared across the room and smashed against the wall. "This is crazy," she told herself. "I have to get Penelope and get out of here."

Clutching the wet doll in her hand, she crawled on her hands and knees towards the kitchen table. About half way there, she stopped. Mom's lemonade pitcher was flying towards her like a rocket. Without a thought, she dove to her right, knocking over the trashcan. "Crash!" the pitcher shattered into a thousand pieces as it hit the pantry door.

When she looked up, she could see Penelope lips moving again. This time she could hear that she was shouting to her. **"Come on, Priscilla. Hurry!"**

Priscilla carefully crawled over the shards of glass until she reached the table. "Are you guys okay?" she asked, almost completely out of breath.

"We're okay. What's happening?" Penelope asked, with tears in her eyes.

"It's the book. We have to get the book. I left it alone upstairs and it's making all of this happen!"

Penelope looked at the doll in her sister's hand. "What are you doing with *that?*"

"I found it out in the snow," Priscilla said, glancing over at a frightened Jasmine.

"What's going on around here?" Jasmine asked, her large brown eyes full of tears.

Priscilla didn't know what to say, so she pretended not to hear the question.

"We have to get out of here—NOW!"

Tears started to flow down Jasmine's face, causing her mascara to run.

"Everything's going to be okay," Penelope said gently. "The cabinets must be almost empty by now. If we wait another minute, it should be safe to come out."

"I can't wait—not even for another minute. I have to get out of this house!" Jasmine screeched, as she darted out from under the table.

"Wait, Jasmine—don't . . . " Penelope's words were carried away with the swirling mass of cheap everyday glassware and blue and yellow stoneware dishes.

"Let her go, Penelope. She'll be all right," said Priscilla.

"But what if she tells people what happened? She could ruin my reputation."

"With everything that has happened, I can't believe that you are still worrying about what other people think.

The only thing that should matter is how you feel about yourself."

Suddenly, the wind began to die down and Priscilla peeked out from under the table. She saw that the tight funnel of the twister had begun to unravel and the contents of the cabinets were now just falling to the floor.

"This is it. Let's go," said Priscilla, grabbing her sister's arm.

As she yanked Penelope out from under the table, her towel fell to the floor, exposing her hideous purple hair. Priscilla fought hard to resist making a joke—they had both been through enough.

Passing through the kitchen doorway, Priscilla felt an immediate sense of calm. She and her sister were out of danger.

"We have to get the book," she said, hesitating just long enough to catch her breath.

"Are you sure that the book is to blame for all of this?" Penelope asked, as she tossed her hair over her shoulder.

"At first I thought that it was Maggie, but as soon as the wind knocked me over, I knew that it was the book."

"But why would the book do something like this?"

"I may be wrong, but I think that all of this was the book's way of getting rid of Jasmine."

A look of disgust came over Penelope's face. "Well, it sure worked." Before heading up the stairs, she took a look in the foyer mirror. "Oh, no—what did she do to my hair? It was supposed to be the color of lavender, not rancid grape juice!"

"Come on—let's go. You can worry about your hair later," Priscilla said, heading for the stairs.

Penelope followed. "Maybe that book will have a spell in it to fix my hair."

"Maybe."

Upstairs in her room, Priscilla noticed that the door to Tikki's cage was open.

"How did that happen?" she said as she ran over to the cage.

Shutting the door, she suddenly realized she hadn't seen her mother since before the cyclone arrived. "Hey, Penelope . . . didn't Mom go into the basement to check the fuse box?"

"You're right, she did. Grab the book and let's go. We have to make sure that she's okay."

Priscilla quickly grabbed the book, which was open and sitting on the bed where she had left it, and the two ran towards the door.

In the basement, the girls found Mom lying on the floor next to a pile of cleaning rags and some cans of old paint.

"Mom . . . are you all right," they cried.

But Mom did not answer. Priscilla, who was holding the book, knelt down on the cold cement floor. Penelope did the same, and the two cradled her body in their hands. "Mom! Wake up . . . it's us!"

Mom groaned softly and then opened her eyes. "What happened?" she asked. "What am I doing down here?"

After the girls helped their mother to her feet, they told her about everything that had happened since the last time they saw her.

"I didn't mean to leave the book alone," Priscilla cried. "I was so pre-occupied with Penelope and Jasmine that I forgot about it."

Mom looked angry. "I'll talk to you both about that later—right now, I want to see the kitchen," she demanded as she headed for the stairs.

Standing in the middle of the kitchen, Mom looked lost. At that moment, Priscilla felt sorry for her mother. She knew how important having a nice home was to her. She could not help but feel that this was all her fault.

"It's all gone," Mom said, looking down at the floor.

Priscilla didn't know what to say.

"How could I have slept through all of this?" Mom asked, as she walked over to the kitchen counter. "What a mess! The book really meant business. Do either of you have any idea why the book would do this?"

"I think that it was the book's way of scaring Jasmine away," Priscilla replied as she walked over to her mother.

"Well, it sure worked," Penelope snapped, as she kicked at the remains of the Santa and Mrs. Claus salt and pepper shakers that Grandma had given them last Christmas. "Jasmine's probably on the phone right now telling everyone what freaks we are."

"I *don't* think so," said a little voice from down below.

Penelope leaped onto a chair as she spotted a furry brown rat on the floor, near her feet.

"Oswald!" said Priscilla, looking down towards the voice. "You shouldn't be in here. You could get hurt!"

"This is the rat that you told me about? You *said* that he spoke to you, but I didn't believe it," Penelope said as she climbed onto the chair, trembling. "I don't like rats!"

"I know how you're feeling. I was scared of him at first, but after we talked, I realized that he was harmless," said Priscilla.

Mom moved closer to Oswald. "How is it that you can talk?"

"The night when the book's magic transformed the house, it also transformed all of its inhabitants."

"What is it that you wanted to tell me?" Priscilla asked her new friend.

"I wanted you to know that Jasmine won't be telling *anyone* what happened."

Penelope cautiously stepped down from the chair. "Why not?" she asked.

Oswald explained how he appeared to Jasmine as she was leaving. "I leapt out in front of her just as she was about to open the door. I really scared her good," he said, chuckling. "Well, anyway, after she backed away from the door, I cornered her against the wall. That's when Maggie came. The walls of the foyer began to glow with a white light so strong I had to cover my eyes. When the light began to fade, I looked up and saw Jasmine pinned against the front door. Her eyes shone like two brand new silver coins and her gaze was fixed on the rays of light. "When you leave this house you will remember nothing. It will be as if this day never happened," Maggie said, and then disappeared back into the walls.

"After Maggie was gone, Jasmine simply left."

"Wow!" said Priscilla. "I didn't know that Maggie could do something that powerful."

Penelope looked up towards the ceiling. "Thank you, Maggie."

"I hope it worked," said Mom.

"I believe in Maggie," said Priscilla. "Remember how she led me to Sarah's doll. That was pretty incredible."

"For all of our sakes, I hope you're right," Mom said as she left the room in search of a couple of brooms.

After the girls thanked Oswald for his help, the clean up began.

An hour later, splatter marks where food had crashed on the kitchen walls and tiled floor were all that remained of the day's events. Standing on a chair, Penelope reached high over her head to clean a gooey red stain from the wall. "Mom, I'm tired. When can we stop for the day?" she asked.

"When we are finished," Mom said sharply.

"Why are you so angry?" Priscilla asked from across the room. She too was standing on a chair cleaning the walls.

"I'm glad that you've asked," replied Mom, as she stepped down from a ladder. "Grandma and I have explained over and over how powerful the magic of the book can be. I'm really disappointed in the both of you."

Priscilla lowered her head. "I know . . . I'm so sorry I left the book alone. It'll *never* happen again."

"I'm sorry too," said Penelope. "I should have been there to help Priscilla."

"That's right, you should have been," said Mom.

"If it helps any, I've learned a huge lesson today," Penelope added.

Mom was quiet for a moment. "Girls, I'm sorry for being so cross. Maybe this is all *my* fault," she said sitting down at the kitchen table. "If I had done things like my mother did, then maybe all of this could have been avoided."

"What do you mean?" asked Priscilla.

"Well, when your grandmother gave the book to me, the first thing we did was make a recipe. It was a good way to introduce me to magic."

Both girls looked at each other.

"If it's okay with you two, I'd like us to make that same recipe," said Mom.

"What kind of recipe?" asked Priscilla.

"It's a surprise," replied Mom.

"Okay," said Priscilla. "But only if you help us."

"Of course I will." Mom replied and then turned to Penelope. "What do you say? Would you like to try a recipe?"

Penelope seemed to be thinking.

Mom rolled her eyes and exhaled loudly. "Penelope—I asked you a question," said Mom. "What do you say? We can't do this without you."

Mom put her arm around Penelope's shoulders.

"Okay, I'll help," Penelope finally said with a sigh.

"Great!" said Mom. "But first I have to go out to get a few things—like bowls for instance. In the meantime, keep working and do not let the book out of your sight."

A few moments later, Mom was gone. When she left, the sun was setting. When she returned an hour later, the black veil of night had arrived.

"Hi, Mom!" Penelope greeted her mother as she walked through the door carrying two large brown shopping bags.

"Did you get what you needed?" Priscilla asked.

"As a matter of fact, I did," replied Mom, carrying the bags into the kitchen.

The girls eagerly followed. Priscilla put the book down on the counter in front of her, and watched closely as Mom carefully removed the contents of the bags. When she was done, the counter was covered from end-to-end with new mixing bowls, a new baking dish, and some strange looking ingredients. There were three small vials filled with colorful powders; a bottle containing a brown liquid; two wooden bowls filled with what looked like waxy rose petals; six tiny round green beads; two green cloth sacks, filled with who knows what; several other unmarked packages, and about a dozen strange purple, plum-like fruits with green thorns.

"Mom—what is all of this for? What are we going to make?" she asked, her eyes wide.

"All of this will be used to make your first recipe from the book, *The Enchanted Snozzleberry Tart,*" Mom said as she opened the book.

"Snozzleberry tart? I never heard of a snozzleberry before," Penelope said, glancing over at the book. "It sounds weird."

"From now on, you're going to encounter a lot of new things—many of which will appear strange at first. I started with this recipe, and so did your grandmother."

Penelope walked over and grabbed one of the vials. "I've never cooked anything in my life," she said. "Well—except for the breakfast that I never finished making."

"I have a feeling that you'll do just fine. Remember . . . you have magic on your side. And besides, I'll be right over there if you really need me," Mom said, smiling as she pointed to the kitchen table.

The girls nodded in agreement.

"Penelope, I think you should prepare the snozzleberries and make the filling for the tart."

Penelope reacted in her usual manner. "You're kidding, right? I don't want to make the filling! I want to do something else!"

Mom responded by telling her to give it a chance.

Penelope paused. "Okay, Mom. I'll give it a try," she said in a huff.

Turning to Priscilla, Mom informed her that it would be her job to make the crust. She agreed without any complaints. She didn't care what part of the recipe was hers to complete. She was just happy to be working out of the book.

After giving her daughters some last words of instruction, Mom sat down at the kitchen table with a magazine. "Now, remember what I said about tasting the tart. The snozzleberries will not be safe to eat until three days after the tart is baked."

"We know!"

"Okay, the first thing I need to do is remove the prickly thorns from the snozzleberries and then wash them well," said Penelope as she picked up and carefully inspected a snozzleberry.

"I'll be right back girls," Mom announced suddenly. "I forgot my glasses upstairs."

"Okay, mom, we'll be fine," replied Priscilla, "but please hurry."

Mom smiled and nodded as she walked out of the room.

As Penelope removed the long thorns, Priscilla began to study her instructions. "This shouldn't be too hard," she said as she picked up a vial of red powder. As she started to add the ingredients to her bowl, she saw the cabinet door in front of her move. At first she thought it was her imagination and returned to her work. A moment later, another cabinet door moved. This time, she put down her wooden mixing spoon and peeked into the cabinet. She saw nothing. Growing annoyed, she decided to open all of the cabinet doors. One-by-one, she threw open each door. "Gotcha!" she said as she peered into the dark and empty wooden compartment.

Beginning to doubt whether or not she saw anything at all, she decided to return to her work. A couple of minutes later as she was mixing the ingredients in her bowl, she saw a softly glowing green light coming from the cabinet above her head. *Not again*, she thought.

Against her better judgment, she once again slowly grabbed the worn handle of the cabinet door. But before she could pull it open all the way, about a dozen brightly glowing fireflies flew out from the opening.

Priscilla stood back and began to smile. "What are you guys doing in there? You frightened me."

Penelope, who had been busy working on removing the snozzleberry thorns, did not notice the fireflies until she heard Priscilla talking.

"What did you say?" she asked, turning around

"Ahhhh! What are those?"

"They're the fireflies that I told you about. There's nothing to be afraid of—they're our friends," Priscilla said as she reached up over her head as if to grab one.

"But why are they glowing green?" Penelope asked, her mouth hanging open.

"It was the book. Remember what I said about its magic being impure?"

"The book again . . . it's always about the book" Penelope whined.

"You're right Penelope. It *is* always about the book . . . and you wait and see, it's also the same book that is going to help our family survive in this town."

Penelope turned away from her sister and resumed her work. Suddenly, a firefly, to whom Priscilla had not yet been formally introduced, flew to the front of the group. "Hello, my name is Jo. Please don't quarrel. You need to come together for everyone's sake. I'm sorry that we frightened you, but we were hiding from that horrible cat. We saw him lurking about in the yard," said the firefly in a gentle voice.

Priscilla reassured the fireflies they were safe in the house and that there was no need to hide. "Don't worry, we'll figure everything out," she said, and the fireflies quickly disappeared through the kitchen door.

Before Priscilla went back to work, she felt that she needed to deal with her sister. "They're gone," she said as she walked up behind Penelope and laid her hand on her shoulder.

Penelope sighed.

Priscilla once again reminded her of what their mother had said about giving the magic a chance. "And don't forget, the book protected us by cloaking the house," she added.

"I hope that you're right," Penelope said finally as she finished adding the remaining ingredients to her bowl.

The kitchen remained quiet for a long time until Penelope let out a loud scream.

"What happened, Penelope? Did you cut yourself or something?" Priscilla asked, rushing over to her sister.

"No—I didn't cut myself! Mashing snozzleberries is hard work. Look—I got berry juice on my dress!" Penelope cried, pointing to the green stain.

"Well, Penelope, you should have changed out of your clothes before we got started."

"I would have if I knew we'd be baking. I had no idea that baking could be so messy."

"Don't complain! You got to do the fun part. I really wanted to mash up the snozzleberries and make the filling."

Penelope thought about their situation for a moment. "I've got an idea. Why don't you help me with the filling when you are done with the crust, and then we can both put the tart in the oven," she said.

Priscilla was surprised, but pleased, by her sister's proposal and offered to help her clean her dress.

"Here—use this. Mom always uses this to clean things," she said, picking up a bottle of dish washing liquid from the counter.

Penelope grabbed the bottle and squeezed a large drop onto the stain. As she began rubbing it with a damp sponge, the stain began to spread. "Priscilla, what did you give me? The stain is spreading—look at my dress!" she wailed.

Just then, Mom returned. "Oh, my goodness, Penelope! What did you two do?" she cried and ran over to her daughter whose hot pink dress was turning snozzleberry green right before their eyes. "What happened?"

"I don't know," wailed Priscilla. "Penelope got some snozzleberry juice on her dress. When I tried to clean it off, the stain spread."

Mom began to smile and grabbed Penelope's hand. "Don't be afraid. This is an unfortunate result of improper snozzleberry mashing," she said. "It happened to me, too, the first time I made this recipe. Except that instead of coloring my clothes, the juice got on Grandma's curtains. Thank goodness Grandma liked the new "green" curtains. Since the color doesn't come out, they might have wound up in the trash."

Priscilla marveled at her mother's calm reaction to what seemed to her to be a horrible incident.

"Now, Penelope, stand perfectly still while the transformation is completed. It will be over in a blink of an eye."

Mom and Priscilla backed away and watched as a bright green glowing wave washed over Penelope's dress.

When it was completely colored, the wave stopped suddenly and, then, *poof*—it was gone.

"See, I told you it wouldn't last long," Mom said as she gave her daughter a hug.

"Penelope, are you okay?" Priscilla asked, as she moved closer.

"I think so."

Penelope's body was still rigid as she looked at her dress. "I can't believe this," she said. "Does this mean that the snozzleberries are a magical fruit?"

"Well, yes," said Mom. "They are."

"I'm glad that you came in when you did," said Priscilla. "Where were you anyway? I thought that you were going to be here in case something like this happened."

Mom sat down at the kitchen table. "I'm sorry girls, I couldn't find my glasses and then when I did, I realized that one of the lenses was missing. After searching the whole upstairs I finally found it in the fireplace room on the sofa. I can't imagine how it got there," Mom said, looking at the book.

"Are you trying to say that the book took the lens out of your glasses and hid it?" asked Priscilla. "Can it do that?"

"I can say from past experience that the book can be mischievous from time to time, especially when it is breaking in its new masters."

"I'll try to remember that," Priscilla said as she looked over at her sister who was now leaning against a chair. "Penelope, are you all right?"

"Honey, why don't you take a break, Mom suggested. "I'll help Priscilla."

"Thanks, I think I need to lie down. But first, I have to take off this dress. Green is definitely not my color," Penelope said as she left the kitchen.

"She looked pretty shaken up," Priscilla said as she resumed work on her dough.

"And that is why I asked her to leave. I think she needs time for all of this to sink in," said Mom. "I hope you don't mind having me as a partner."

"Of course not!"

Twenty minutes later, Priscilla let out a triumphant "Ta Dah! The dough is ready to be rolled."

"That's great, honey," Mom replied from the other end of the counter.

But as Priscilla pushed the rolling pin over the dough, it stuck to everything—her fingers, the rolling pin, and the pastry board was covered with wet sticky dough. "What happened? I tried to follow the directions perfectly."

Mom came over and tasted the dough. "It's okay, honey, I think it just needs a little more Reubil flour."

Priscilla sighed. "I thought I'd measured it correctly," she said, grabbing the green sack containing the flour. "How much should I add?"

Before Mom could answer, Penelope came through the kitchen door. This time, she was wearing black leggings and a pink blouse. "I just wanted to let you know that I was feeling better," she said, staring at Priscilla's sticky hands, which were dripping dough onto the floor. "What happened to the dough?"

Mom explained how Priscilla didn't add enough flour.

"I'm sure we'll both do a better job next time," Penelope said as she looked at the recipe again.

Mom gave Penelope a gentle hug. "You're doing better than you think. So much so that I trust that you two can handle finishing the recipe. I'll be upstairs if you need me," she said as she grabbed her magazine off the table. "I've already mashed the snozzleberries properly, so you don't have to worry about the juice again."

"What do you mean, you're leaving? I thought you were going to stay and help us. We need you," Priscilla said as she grabbed her mother's hand.

"Yeah, Mom—I don't think I could handle another incident like the last one," Penelope said nervously.

Mom put her arms around her daughters. "I know that you can, and you will. Just remember that no matter what happens, the magic won't harm you."

Mom headed towards the door.

"I'd really feel much better if you stayed," said Penelope.

"Please trust that I have good reasons for leaving, all of which are for the good of your training," Mom replied and left the room.

"Can you believe her? First she tells us that she'll be here for us, and then she leaves," whined Penelope.

"It sounds like you're feeling better," Priscilla said, grabbing a measuring cup.

Penelope smiled. "What choice do I have? If you want, I can help you finish making the dough."

Priscilla smiled back. "Okay, but first I'll help you finish making the filling."

As the two started to gather the ingredients for the filling, Priscilla heard a scratching noise coming from the window. When she glanced over her shoulder, she saw Pumpkin spring from the window into the nearby tree. "Penelope, look! I just saw Pumpkin. I think he was watching us."

Both girls rushed to the window.

"I don't see him," said Penelope. "But, if you're right, I bet that he's on his way back to give his report to Mrs. Maven." She slumped down at the kitchen table and added, "We have to do something about that cat."

Priscilla returned to the counter. "I agree! Later— after we finish the tart—we'll figure out something."

Penelope nodded and returned to the counter. "I'm ready to finish the filling. Are you ready to help me?"

Priscilla smiled. "Of course—don't forget, this was supposed to be a team effort."

Penelope proceeded to wrap one of Mom's aprons around her waist, while Priscilla grabbed a dishtowel and slung it over her shoulder. Penelope took the bowl of mashed berries and brought it over to the other ingredients. Priscilla began to pour in the right amounts of green beads, colored powders, and waxy leaves. Slowly, Penelope began to mix the ingredients together. Suddenly, something odd started to happen. Each new ingredient began to dance and swirl around and around blending with the others. Penelope stepped back, trembling. Priscilla also took a step back.

"What's happening now?" cried Penelope.

Once again, Priscilla stepped up to the bowl. "I think that the book is trying to help us." As she bent down to take a closer look, the mixture began to bubble and gurgle-like a mini volcano. "I think it's going to blow," she said, backing away and shielding her face.

When the bubbling and gurgling finally stopped a few minutes later, the girls slowly approached the bowl and peered inside.

"I think it's safe now—I guess it's done," said Priscilla.

"It's more than done, it's beautiful!" replied Penelope, her eyes wide and trance-like as she stared into the bowl. Then she smiled. "Can you see how all the ingredients have blended to make this beautiful tapestry of texture and color?"

Priscilla gave her sister a curious look. *What has gotten into her? Penelope appears to be happier than I've seen her in a long time.*

Taking a spoon, Penelope cautiously gave the filling a final twirl, put the spoon to her lips, and then remembered her mother's warning—she resisted the impulse to taste it. "I wonder if the filling tastes as good as it looks!"

The crust was next. Penelope helped Priscilla measure out the exact amount of Reubil flour from the green cloth sack. They followed the directions very carefully, and to Priscilla's delight, this time, the crust rolled out perfectly.

Penelope added the filling and together the girls put the tart in the oven to bake. As Priscilla was about to close the oven door, she felt a tingling on the back of her arms and neck. "Penelope, do you feel that?" she said.

"If you mean the tickling sensation on the back of my neck—yeah."

Both girls slowly turned around. Priscilla was almost afraid of what she might see. To her great surprise, someone or something had cleaned up the mess in the kitchen while their backs were turned. Looking at each other, they both said, "The book!"

About an hour later, the tart came out of the oven and it looked delicious.

"Magic or no magic, I think that we did a great job," said Penelope.

For the first time in a long time, Priscilla recognized a glimmer of the old Penelope. *Maybe everything is going to be okay,* she thought to herself.

Mom came into the kitchen shortly afterwards. "Hey, that smells delicious," she said as she bent down to smell the tart.

"Thanks!" replied Penelope. "I can't believe it—we really did it."

Mom smiled. "I knew that you could."

"What do we do now? We don't even know what this tart does," asked Priscilla.

"First, we have to cover it. The rest you'll find out in three days when we taste it. I thought that you liked surprises?" Mom replied as she laid the tart on a fancy crystal dish and covered it with a sparkling crystal lid. "It's a good thing that I kept this set in the dining room hutch."

Priscilla smiled, but Penelope had a far off look on her face.

"What would happen if we ate the tart before the snozzleberries are ripe?" Penelope asked suddenly.

Mom's upper lip started to quiver. "Don't even joke about that," she replied.

The girls looked at each other.

"I wasn't joking," Penelope muttered and turned away.

Mom said nothing, leaving Priscilla to assume that her mother hadn't heard her sister.

After a moment of uncomfortable silence, Mom spoke as she rifled through the refrigerator. "So, did anything happen while you were finishing the recipe?"

Without hesitation, Penelope told her mother everything that had happened.

"And this is the reason why I left you two alone," Mom said. "I knew there would be more magic and I didn't want you to rely on me to help you deal with it. I won't always be there to tell you what to do, so you have to learn to think for yourselves. Was my plan successful? Did either of you learn anything about yourselves?"

The girls looked at each other.

"I think so," said Priscilla smiling. "We worked well together, and I think that Penelope is starting to like magic."

Mom smiled at Penelope. "Really, Penelope?" she asked.

"It was strange—for the first time in a long time I wasn't afraid. When I looked into the bowl and saw the magic, I felt it inside me. I felt a warmth travel through my body like an electrical surge. And I felt really happy. When the mixture stopped bubbling, I felt the warm feeling leave me and I was a little sad. Mom—I think I might be ready to learn more."

Mom hugged her girls. "This is wonderful. Consider this your first official lesson. Now, class dismissed. You both need to get ready for bed—it's getting late, and I've got to call Grandma," she said, reaching for the telephone.

Chapter Twelve

Penelope Begins to Find Herself

On their way to school the following Monday, the sisters chattered away about the events that occurred over the weekend.

"We really did it! I wonder what else we can do!" Penelope exclaimed as she skipped alongside her sister.

"I don't know, but I'm sure we'll find out soon enough. Eventually, we are going to have to do something about Pumpkin," Priscilla replied. "We can't have him nosing around while we're performing spells."

Penelope agreed.

As the girls crossed the street and came up on Mrs. Maven's house, they quickened their pace. Once past the house, they slowed down again.

"I wish she would just move away," said Penelope.

"I agree—and the sooner the better," said a soft voice.

Penelope looked around but saw no one. Then, she looked up to see a tiny green glowing firefly fluttering above her head. Unsure what to say, she nudged her sister. "Look Priscilla, it's one of your friends," she said, pointing to the firefly.

"You mean one of our friends. Willow, is that you?"

When the firefly spoke, her voice was faint.

Penelope realized that her tiny friend was almost completely out of breath.

"I have something . . . to tell you. I was on my way home last night from my midnight flight when . . . I passed by Mrs. Maven's house. I saw something that made me stop."

Penelope held her breath.

"Mrs. Maven was sitting out on her porch talking to Pumpkin. He told her that he could provide her with the evidence that she's been after. That's when he mentioned the book. He plans to steal it from your house after school today."

"I can't believe it! Who does that cat think he is? Does he think that I'm going to just leave the book lying around next to an open window?" Priscilla ranted.

"Hey! Wait a minute. I've got an idea!" exclaimed Penelope. "Why don't we give him what he wants?"

"**Are you crazy?**" Priscilla shouted.

"Wait! Hear me out. We can use Oswald to lure Pumpkin over to our house. We can set the book on, say, the porch. We'll be in the bushes waiting. When he tries to take the book, we can cast some sort of spell on him that would rid us of him forever."

Priscilla looked stunned. "You came up with that just now?" she asked.

"Yeah! I'm even surprising myself!"

"It sounds like a good plan, but what kind of spell should we do?"

"I don't know yet, but we'll find one. Let's go—we don't have much time. We can go back home and look through the book."

Priscilla agreed, and the three turned around and headed back to the house. Penelope did not like to skip school, but she felt that there could be no better reason than this.

Back home, Mom had already left for work and the house was quiet. Priscilla plopped down on the parlor sofa and opened her backpack. "I don't know how much longer I can lug this thing around," she sighed as she pulled out the book.

"Would you mind if I stayed here for a bit?" Willow asked from overhead and yawned. "I'm so tired."

"Of course not, you can stay with us for as long as you want," replied Priscilla.

Willow flashed her green glowing light and fluttered over to Priscilla's shoulder where she landed. Priscilla smiled at her and opened the book.

"How do you think we'll know when we've controlled the book?" Penelope asked, sitting down next to her sister.

"I don't know," Priscilla replied, quickly flipping the pages. "First we need to focus on the spell—let's start with the *Recipes*."

Again, she began to flip through the book. The pages began to glisten like the sun kissed ripples of a gently flowing stream. She found the sight soothing. For an instant, she was hypnotized.

"Earth to Priscilla," Penelope said, snapping her fingers in front of her sister's face.

With a jerk, Priscilla came around. "What happened?" she asked, looking down at the book.

"I'm not sure—you spaced out for a couple of seconds."

Priscilla pointed to the open page before her. "Look, what about this one? It's called *Olive Wart*."

Penelope made a face. "That's disgusting!"

The two sisters read the recipe.

"No, this one's not right! Even though I wouldn't mind giving him a bad case of giant toad warts, we still wouldn't be rid of him," said Penelope.

Priscilla moved on to the next recipe and Penelope read the title. "This one is called *Sloan's Revenge*. It sounds even worse than the last one."

"I know! Look at the ingredients—pickled dandelion buds and salted bug slime . . . one big yuck!"

"Don't forget this delightful one—*Vallenroot Surprise*. I wonder what the surprise is—maybe that it tastes good."

On the next page, the girls found the recipe for *The Enchanted Snozzleberry Tart*.

"Hurry! Read the part that tells us what the recipe is for," Penelope cried.

"That's strange," said Priscilla, squinting her eyes. "It doesn't say anything—it's blank."

"That is strange. There's a place for the information, but the information is missing," Penelope observed. "I guess that we'll have to wait for Mom to tell us."

"You know—I don't think that any of these are right. Let's look at the next section titled *Spells*," suggested Priscilla.

Priscilla began to flip through dozens of spells. "There are some interesting ones in here."

"Hey, wait! Take a look at this one," Penelope said as she pointed to a spell that read *The Winkler Tinkler Enabler Spell*.

Priscilla read the page. "The book says that this spell is supposed to enhance a mortal's or a beast's natural abilities. It can even cause them to become superhuman."

Penelope shook her head. "I don't think we want to make Pumpkin superhuman."

Priscilla giggled. "I agree," she said and continued to flip. "Here we have *The Slug Prognosticating Spell* and *The Belch Slime Return Spell.*"

Penelope cringed. "None of those sound right," she whined.

When Priscilla turned to the next page, something magical happened. The words on the page lit up like a neon sign.

"**This is it—this must be the one!**" Penelope shouted, startling her sister. "The book is showing us that this is the one!"

"I think you're right, but I can't read it—the light is too bright."

Penelope squinted. The light emanating from the book *was* too bright. "My eyes are beginning to hurt. I'm gonna go upstairs and get my sunglasses," she said as she ran towards the stairs.

"Could you get mine too—they're on my dresser."

Penelope agreed, and when she returned, the two read from the page.

"It's called *The Garden Sludge Beetle Minimizer Spell,*" Priscilla announced.

"The spell is perfect, except we need a lot of strange ingredients. Where are we going to get a thistle root, and what is a wooly-backed beetle?" Penelope asked nervously.

"I'm not sure, but I think I saw something that resembled a root in the pantry. I'll bet we'll find most of the things we need in there. I think Mom bought additional items when she shopped for the tart ingredients," Priscilla said as she placed Willow on the sofa's backrest, stood up, and ran to the kitchen.

She returned a few minutes later holding a root about as long as a fly swatter and striped like a traditional red and white candy cane.

"What is *that?*"

"What do you *think?*"

"How do you know that it's a thistle root?"

Priscilla explained the root was in a bag labeled *Thistle Root.*

Penelope smiled and said, "You've got a good eye."

"And a good nose, too. This thing really stinks!"

"I know what you mean," Penelope said, wrinkling her nose. "It reminds me of Grandma's cure-all soup."

Priscilla giggled. "By the way, I was right. There are a lot of things in there that we can use," she said excitedly.

"Great!" replied Penelope.

"Hey—what's that?" Priscilla asked, pointing to the open page on Penelope's lap.

"It's the *Secrets* section of the book. I thought that it might contain some juicy gossip or something."

Priscilla sat down on the sofa and together the two scoured the third section of the book.

"This is interesting," said Priscilla, pointing to a picture of three wolves digging a deep hole in the ground.

> *"Beneath the land of many runs wide-open spaces hidden from view or knowledge exists a world in itself."*

"That's not a secret at all. It's more like a riddle!" exclaimed Penelope. "I wonder what it all means."

"I'm sure that Mom must know. She had the book before us."

Penelope looked at her watch. "It's getting late. We had better get going if we're going to do all of this before Mom gets home. It would be great if we could surprise her."

"Wait a minute," Priscilla said grabbing her sister's arm. "There's one more thing that I would like to look up, but I have to tell you a few things first."

"What's wrong?"

Priscilla told her sister about Mrs. Willowby, the Samuels, and Sarah.

"I'm glad that you finally told me. Maybe we should look in the book to see if it says anything about the doll."

"Sister . . . I think you just read my mind," Priscilla said, and the two flipped through the book.

"There's nothing here," Priscilla said, disappointed. "I'm going to call Maggie to see if she can help us." She stood up and called out to her friend. "My friend, I need your help. Trouble is coming. Pumpkin is going to try to steal the book."

A moment later, the wind began to howl and the walls shook. Penelope moved closer to her sister.

"What's happening?" she asked nervously.

"Don't be afraid. That's just Maggie. She sounds scary, but she's really very gentle."

While the two waited for Maggie, Penelope, now in possession of a new enthusiasm, asked Priscilla who she thought Mrs. Willowby really was.

"Boy, Penelope—you'd better watch out or someone might think that you're starting to enjoy all of this."

"It's strange, but ever since we made the tart, I feel differently towards magic," Penelope whispered.

Priscilla smiled, and the two of them looked up at the ceiling and waited. A minute later, a soft voice surrounded them like the soft sound of a foghorn on a distant bay. "What is it that you need, my friends?" Maggie whispered.

Priscilla stood up and explained their problem.

"I too have seen that cat about. I will call upon Oswald right away," replied Maggie.

It wasn't long before Oswald appeared in the foyer, scratching his belly and licking his tiny hands. "Hi, guys! I'm sorry that I took so long, but if I don't eat every two hours, I feel faint."

"That's okay, Oswald. We were just working on a spell," Penelope said.

Priscilla told Oswald about the problem with Pumpkin and asked for his help.

"Of course I'll help. I'll get the fireflies too. That cat has been chasing me for far too long."

While Oswald was gone the girls headed into the kitchen to discuss, over potato chips and orange juice, the roles their friends would play in their plan.

"But how will Oswald bring the book to us? He's only a rat and the book is very heavy," Penelope inquired.

"Well, maybe he can drag it if we tie, say, a string or something around his waist," replied Priscilla thoughtfully.

"You've got to be kidding! He's not strong enough! Penelope replied in disbelief.

Priscilla took another bite out of her chip and stared down at the open book in front of her.

Penelope sensed that her sister was concentrating on a solution to their problem—she hoped that she would come up with something quickly.

Priscilla began turning the pages, back to a spell they had previously dismissed, and announced, "This is it! We're going to perform a spell that will give Oswald the strength to carry the book."

Penelope looked stunned. *"The Winkler Tinkler Enabler Spell?* I don't know, Priscilla. What if something goes wrong? What if it doesn't work?

"It'll work! Trust me! I have a feeling about this. With this spell, Oswald will have the strength of a hundred rats," Priscilla announced confidently.

Penelope gnawed on her lip as she took a few minutes to think things over. Looking her sister in the eye she asked, finally, "What do we have to do?"

The girls headed back to the parlor and together they read the spell again. When Oswald finally returned with the fireflies, Penelope asked for his permission to perform the spell. "The effects aren't permanent, and we promise to be careful."

Oswald twitched his nose and puffed out his chest. "Are you sure you can't make it permanent? With super powers, I can show all the cats in the neighborhood who's the boss. I'll have the pick of garbage cans."

Penelope and Priscilla smiled at each other, and even though they restated that the spell would only be temporary, Oswald agreed to do whatever he could to help his friends.

Everyone gathered around the book to receive their instructions. "We'd better get started. There's so much to do," Penelope said as she motioned to the fireflies to exit out the window she had opened. She grabbed the book and headed toward the kitchen. Priscilla, who was carrying Oswald, was right behind her. When they were finished performing the spell, Oswald disappeared through an opening near the stairs.

Priscilla grabbed the book and an old pillowcase from the laundry room, into which she placed an odd assortment of ingredients: a cup of toilet water, one broken light bulb, the thirteenth eye of a dried attic-dwelling wooly-backed beetle, a day-old banana peel, a pinch of black pepper, a handful of dried thistle root, two slices of moldy cheese, and a hair from the intended victim—Pumpkin. She followed Penelope outside.

The sun was shining and the air felt too warm for February. Like escaped convicts, the girls crouched down in the bushes to the left of the porch steps. Penelope propped the book up on her knee. "Do you really think that we can do this?" she asked, biting her lip again.

"I think so," Priscilla replied, her voice unwavering. "We don't have any choice—we have to try."

"Well, if it doesn't work, maybe the book will take pity on us and scare Pumpkin away like Maggie did with Jasmine," Penelope said with a grin as she handed the book to Priscilla.

Priscilla chuckled and opened the book up to *The Garden Sludge Beetle Minimizer Spell*. But before they could prepare for the spell, Penelope heard muffled voices coming from somewhere across the street and they seemed to be getting louder. Quickly, she grabbed the book from her sister. "I'll put it on the porch," she whispered and hurried away.

The short distance to the porch seemed to take minutes instead of its actual time of five seconds. Penelope carefully placed the book down on the porch and crept back to the bush. To her surprise, Priscilla was gone. "Priscilla, where are you?" she whispered.

"I'm over here," Priscilla whispered from the bush to Penelope's left.

"What are you doing?" Penelope asked following the sound of thumping and crunching.

As she entered a small opening in the massive spiked evergreen, she saw her sister jumping up and down on the pillowcase as part of the preparation process.

"Why did you move?" Penelope asked, inching closer.

Priscilla stopped jumping and explained to her sister how she had seen Pumpkin and thought that he had seen her hiding in the bush. "Before I could think, my feet were moving," she explained.

Penelope smoothed her hair. "Okay—I guess we can finish preparing the spell here, but we really need to get back to the other bush so we can see the porch."

"All right," Priscilla said, picking up the muddy pillowcase.

Penelope watched as her sister removed a small bottle from her coat pocket.

"I almost forgot to add the Beridium," Priscilla announced.

"Is that the last ingredient?" Penelope inquired as she took note of the expression on her sister's face. *She seems to really be enjoying all of this. Maybe we have a chance to be a real team after all,* she thought.

"Yeah, the last and the most important. Without the Beridium, this sack of potentially powerful potion would be no more than a muddy, wet, and smelly pillowcase," Priscilla said as she held the pillowcase out to Penelope. "Here—hold this while I add the Beridium."

While Penelope did as asked, Priscilla slowly poured in half the brown liquid. The pillowcase began to jump and move as if filled with a dozen angry snakes. Penelope became frightened and dropped the pillowcase to the ground. "I know that this is all part of the spell, but I'm scared," she said, her hands trembling.

Priscilla shoved the bottle of Beridium into her pocket and picked up the pillowcase. "Don't worry—it'll stop in a few seconds," she replied, taking a peek into the dark sack.

"What do you see?" Penelope asked timidly.

"It's really cool—take a look," Priscilla whispered.

Penelope took a deep breath and peered into the pillowcase. She was shocked and only a little frightened to see the root powder thrashing around with the Beridium and the other ingredients Priscilla had added earlier. All of a sudden, the pillowcase became still.

"Great! It's done!" Priscilla announced.

Penelope felt relieved and took note of the calm that seemed to surround her.

A moment later, the calm was replaced by the high-pitched chattering of the fireflies announcing the approach of Oswald and Pumpkin. **"They're coming . . . they're coming. They've just crossed Second Avenue."**

"Thanks, guys," Priscilla said as the fireflies flew over their heads and disappeared. Now, the voices of Oswald and Pumpkin were heard clearly.

"I'm going to catch you, my friend—and, when I do, I'm going to have my master boil you in fish oil so that I can eat you!" roared Pumpkin.

"You're not so scary without your teeth, my old friend. I know that you can't hurt me. Besides, I have a surprise for you."

"Here's our chance to get back to the other bush," Penelope whispered.

Priscilla nodded and grabbed the pillowcase. "I've got it."

A moment later, the two were back safely inside the bush near the steps. Penelope parted some branches just in time to see Oswald leap onto the front porch, followed by Pumpkin, who landed with his front paws on the book. "What's *this*? Have those silly girls actually left the book unguarded?" he asked with his dirty, matted hair standing up on his back.

But before he could move even one of those hairs, Oswald came up behind him and pulled the book right out from under him.

"**Hey! Where are you going with my book?**" Pumpkin screeched.

Penelope did not see where Oswald had gone, but she knew that he'd be along with the book shortly. Within seconds he appeared scampering towards them from the front lawn. A thick piece of cord was tied around his waist and he dragged the heavy book behind him.

"It worked! It really worked!" Penelope whispered as she peered out from the bush.

"I told you so!" Priscilla replied, leaning over her sister's shoulder. "Here he comes!"

Once inside the bush, Oswald stopped next to the pillowcase, his furry little chest bobbing up and down like a buoy on a turbulent sea. "Hi, guys! How did I do?"

"Great job!" Penelope said, "You're incredible."

"So are you guys. So far, so good."

Priscilla removed the cord from both the book and Oswald, and then as he backed away he whispered, ".Good luck!"

Trembling slightly, Priscilla began to chant.

"I ask from you great Abisius that you grant us the immense power of the book. We come together with the book to ask for the power of the Enlightened Ones to fill us."

Penelope slowly reached her hand into the pillowcase and grabbed a handful of the magic powder—it poured through her fingers like sand as she handed it to Priscilla.

*"From now to then, from big to small, we ask the
forces of nature to help protect the Enlightened Ones
for the good of our people, and for all people, remake
this creature. Accept our offering, accept our plea."*

As Priscilla attempted to finish the spell, Pumpkin
came bounding through the bushes, heading right for her.

"**Perfect!**" she yelled, with fire in her eyes.

"**Finish it**!" cried Penelope.

"Change this cat to the size of a flea."

Before she uttered the last word, Priscilla launched
the white powder in Pumpkin's direction. When the powder
touched the unsuspecting feline's fur, a translucent cloud rose
up in the air and hundreds of tiny sparks popped and sizzled.
The air around the girls was beginning to heat up, stinging
their faces, and causing them to turn away. A few seconds
later, particles resembling silver glitter began to rain down
upon them and the cloud disappeared—Pumpkin was no
where to be found.

"Wow, that was incredible! Do you think it worked?"
Penelope asked glancing down at her dirty clothes.

"Well, something definitely happened. That was
awesome! It made *The Winkler Tinkler Enabler Spell* look like a
snooze-fest," Priscilla replied, rubbing her eyes.

"I wouldn't go that far, but this was definitely some
potent magic."

As the girls searched the grounds for Pumpkin,
Oswald retired to the house for a long overdue nap.

"How big is a garden sludge beetle anyway?" Priscilla
asked as she crept around in the flowerbed.

"I'm not sure, but I guess that it's pretty small. That's probably why we can't find him," Penelope replied, glancing down at the ground. "What's this?" she asked, removing a piece of fluorescent pink paper from the bottom of her boot.

"What is it?" Priscilla asked as she came up behind her sister.

"It's a flyer inviting all of the residents of Dunville to attend a meeting at Mrs. Maven's house tonight," Penelope replied. As she read the paper, her face started to turn as green as an un-ripened banana.

Priscilla, looking over her sister's shoulder, began to read aloud:

> THERE ARE MENACING FORCES LIVING
> AMONG US. GATHER TOGETHER AND
> JOIN ME AT MY HOUSE TONIGHT AT 8PM.
> BE THERE OR BE FOOLED!
>
> MRS. MAVEN
>
> Refreshments will be served

When Priscilla was finished, she almost dropped the book. "**I can't believe it—she's finally done it!**" she shouted. "**That crazy old woman is finally going public!**"

Penelope's natural color slowly returned. "I bet that she was planning to parade our book around at this meeting," she said.

"It's a good thing that we stopped Pumpkin, but I'm still worried. We can't let Mrs. Maven have that meeting. If even one person shows up and buys into her crazy talk, we could be in real danger." Priscilla crumpled up the flyer and asked, "So what do we do now?"

"I think that we should wait for Mom to get home. Pumpkin was one thing . . . I don't think that we can handle Mrs. Maven by ourselves," Penelope replied, heading towards the house.

The hours seemed to drag until Mom returned home. She had no sooner walked in the door when the girls began to explain how they found out about Pumpkin's plan to steal the book, and confessed to shrinking him to the size of a small bug.

"We were protecting the family. We wanted you to be proud of us," Priscilla explained.

Mom's nostrils flared, and the point between her eyebrows turned red. These were two unmistakable signs that she was both agitated and confused. "**You girls shouldn't have attempted the spell alone—you're not experienced enough yet!**" she shouted.

"But the spell worked," Priscilla replied triumphantly.

"You said it yourself —you couldn't find Pumpkin. You don't know that it worked," Mom replied in a shaky voice.

Priscilla fell down on the sofa, dropping her head into her hands. Penelope sat down too, but Mom remained standing with her arms crossed in front of her. After a few minutes of quietly staring at the floor, Penelope spoke. "Mom, there's another problem."

Mom sighed heavily and waited for her daughter to continue. Penelope told her mother about the flyer and her suspicion that Mrs. Maven was going to display their book at the meeting.

"I see now that she's more dangerous than we thought, but I don't know what we can do to stop her. You might as well learn right now that you can't always turn to magic to solve your problems," said Mom.

No one said a word. Penelope thought that it was strange that her sister didn't argue. She knew that she was up to something.

"Mom, you and Grandma said that the intent of the book was to do good and to help people. What's wrong with us using it to protect ourselves? If someone doesn't do something about Mrs. Maven, life as we know it will be over," Priscilla said finally.

Mom was quiet. She was always quiet when she was considering something. "What did you have in mind?" she asked suddenly.

"I haven't had much time to think about it, but what about the first spell that the book showed us?" Priscilla replied. "It's a transformation spell. Maybe we can use it to turn Mrs. Maven into a nice person."

Mom was quiet for a moment and then let out another big sigh. "That's a very powerful spell. You are both way too inexperienced. I didn't attempt that spell until I was 17," she protested. "What if I go and talk to her . . . maybe I can convince her."

Penelope interrupted. "Trust us, Mom, it won't do any good. We've talked to her. She's irrational."

"Have you forgotten your own rule about not going near her alone?" added Priscilla.

Mom nodded and after a few minutes spoke. "Your grandmother would have me thrown in a ditch and left there for the coyotes if she knew about this, but okay . . . let's do the spell. But we have to act quickly."

Penelope gave her mother a big hug.

"The first thing that we need to do is to go over the spell. After we do that, I will go out and retrieve the necessary ingredients. While I'm away, it will be your job, Priscilla, to summon Maggie and her friends," said Mom.

Priscilla grabbed the book and followed Mom and Penelope into the den. Penelope thought that Mom and Priscilla looked awfully serious. *The last time I saw either of them look that way was the day we moved to Dunville.*

Walking into the room, she couldn't help but think about all the times she and her dad sat on that brown leather couch reading her favorite books. She also loved to sit on it, wrapped up in Grandma's old rag quilt. She couldn't help but think that this was the perfect place for studying spells.

The sound of Mom's voice brought Penelope back to the present. "This spell can be dangerous if done incorrectly. You must both follow my directions at all times," she warned.

"We will," said both girls.

"We'll make you proud," Priscilla added.

Mom asked Priscilla to read the spell out loud, and then she assigned each daughter her role. Twenty minutes later, everyone sat down to an early dinner of turkey sandwiches and lemonade, but Penelope could not eat a bite. She was pretty nervous about performing the spell. At about four-thirty, Mom put on her coat. "I'll be back in one hour. Are you sure that you both understand what you need to do?" she asked.

Both girls nodded and followed their mother to the front door.

"Good Luck," Penelope said and then turned and went into the parlor.

Priscilla joined her there a couple of minutes later.

Sitting on the sofa, Penelope went over the spell in her head until she felt confident she knew what she was supposed to do.

As discussed in the den, when the clock struck five, Priscilla called out to Maggie.

This time, she came more quickly than in the past, and was happy to help. Penelope figured that her walls not only had eyes, but ears as well.

"Of course I will help," Maggie howled like the wind, and offered to call upon her friends.

An hour later, Oswald, Willow, and the rest of the fireflies joined the girls in the kitchen. As Priscilla filled them in on the plan, Mom came in carrying a bulging, brown paper bag. Ready to drop the overfilled bag, she set it down on the counter with a low *thump*.

"Did you get everything that we need?" Penelope asked, sitting down at the table.

"I was lucky. I got the last crystal jar in the shop."

Penelope wondered what sort of store sold such things as enchanted crystal jars.

"I am pleased to see that we have such good friends living among us," Mom said, turning to Oswald. "We could not do this alone."

With that said, Mom put a wedge under the kitchen door to keep it open. Next, she grabbed the bag and motioned for Priscilla to pick up the book, and then led the girls into the dark and cramped pantry.

"Why do we have to do the spell here?" Penelope whined.

"I already told you Penelope—this is the safest place for us. And besides, from here, we can see everything—all around the kitchen and even into the foyer," Mom replied as she lit a small white taper candle that she took from her pocket.

"And let there be light," Priscilla said and giggled nervously.

After Mom set the candle on a shelf, she pulled a piece of what looked like beat up zebra fur from the paper bag. "Priscilla—you hold this very gently," she said.

Priscilla took the fur and held it up between her thumb and index finger. "I didn't think that it would be quite so ragged," she said.

Penelope gasped when she saw the fur and was grateful it wasn't handed to her.

Next, Mom removed a glowing crystal jar from the bag. "Be very careful with this," she told Penelope. "If it breaks, terrible things will happen."

Penelope accepted the jar and cradled it in her arms like a newborn baby.

"It's okay, honey! You don't have to hold it the whole time. I need you to keep watch," Mom whispered.

Penelope gently placed the jar on a shelf next to her and returned to her post. Peering out from the cracked door, she realized her mother was right. She could see the front door from there. As she peered out into the empty kitchen, her stomach began to churn. "What am I doing?" she asked herself.

At a quarter to six, Priscilla whistled for Willow and the rest of the fireflies. It was their job to deliver a note to Mrs. Maven. The note stated that they were holding Pumpkin hostage and that Mrs. Maven should come to their house at six o'clock sharp if she wanted him back.

A few minutes later, Willow appeared in the kitchen doorway followed by ten of her closest firefly friends. Like a tiny insect army, the troop flew close together and moved as a well-trained unit. Penelope noticed that their softly glowing green lights had even darkened to a drab army-green color.

Like an insect squad of paratroopers Willow and three of her firefly friends landed on the kitchen table. Together, they hoisted the letter onto their backs and carried it off towards the front door. Five minutes later they returned, confirming the delivery.

"Great! Now, all we have to do is wait," Mom said as Priscilla opened the book to the transformation spell.

At approximately six o'clock, the doorbell rang. Penelope peered out from the pantry door. "I think it's her."

There was a loud banging on the door that grew louder and louder with each bang. It was as if someone was hitting the door with a rock.

"She's trying to break the door down!" Mom cried.

The banging stopped and, magically, the door sprang open as if an invisible doorman had come back from his break.

"Good going, Maggie," Penelope whispered.

"I wish that I could see," Priscilla began to complain. "What's happening now? Is it her?" she asked, holding onto her mother's arm.

"It's her," Penelope reported as she watched Mrs. Maven walk through the door.

Not yet through, the old woman stopped and began to sway back and forth like a young tree in a strong wind.

"I think she's drunk," Penelope whispered. "Do you think Alcohol will affect the spell?"

"I don't think so, but then again, magic can be sensitive to any changes within the body," replied Mom.

"That doesn't make me feel any better."

"Sorry!"

As Mrs. Maven stumbled towards the kitchen, she would periodically stop and sway.

189

"Just when I think that she's going down, those legs hold firm to the floor like giant building supports," Penelope mumbled over her shoulder.

"What are you talking about?" Priscilla grumbled as she started to move forward.

"Where do you think you're going?" Mom asked, grabbing the back of Priscilla's shirt.

"I want to see what's happening. Why does she get to see everything?"

"Because I assigned that job to her, that's why!" Mom snapped.

"Fine!" Priscilla said and sat back down

When Mrs. Maven neared the stairs, she tripped on the hallway runner. "**THUMP!**" She hit the floor with the force of a bowling ball.

"Darn rug! Who puts rugs . . . on the floor where decent people walk . . . anyway?" she slurred.

As Mrs. Maven struggled to get up, a piece of crumpled paper fell from the pocket of her long, tattered gray sweater-vest. Penelope assumed that it was their note.

"Where is everyone? I have a note . . . it says that you have my cat." As Mrs. Maven spoke, she continued to slur her words, and small pools of drool glistened around her mouth.

The house was so quiet that Penelope could hear the woman's labored breathing, as well as the creaking of the floors under her enormous weight.

"Hey, everyone! It's Oswald!" Penelope said suddenly. "He's heading towards Mrs. Maven. I don't think she sees him."

"*Squeak, squeak, squeak!*" Oswald spat as he jumped up onto her leg.

Mrs. Maven screamed. "Send your rat to attack me will you," she said, shaking the creature from her leg.

Oswald hit the floor with a soft *thud*. When he got up, he rubbed his back and stuck his tongue out at Mrs. Maven before scurrying away.

"She's coming this way," whispered Penelope.

Everyone held still.

"Are you both ready? We have to act quickly," said Mom.

Penelope turned around and picked up the jar.

"Are you sure this is big enough to fit her?" Priscilla asked.

Mom motioned for her to be quiet.

"She's in the kitchen," said Penelope, starting to tremble.

Penelope turned around and saw that Priscilla was starting to tremble too. As Priscilla opened the book, Mom lit a second candle that she had removed from her pocket.

"Where is everyone? Where is my cat?" Mrs. Maven demanded, stomping her foot on the floor. "I am tired of waiting." Standing in the middle of the kitchen, she suspiciously glanced around the room. "I know that you're here. I can sense you," she hissed.

"What does she mean she can *sense* us?" Priscilla whispered.

"Shhh!" said Mom.

Penelope continued to peek out the door.

Mrs. Maven walked over to the tart. "What do we have here? It looks like the witches have made themselves a little dessert," she said.

"Mom, she's lifting the cover off the tart," Penelope whispered.

"Let's just do it already," said Priscilla.

Mom did not respond right away, but appeared to be thinking. "Wait!" she said suddenly.

Penelope held her breath for just a second. "She's going to eat the tart!" she cried, turning to her mother who was now smiling.

Suddenly, Mom squeezed past Priscilla and crawled over to the door. "Excuse me, Penelope. I want to see what's happening for myself." Peering out from the door, she suddenly said, "Let her eat it!"

The girls looked at each other.

Penelope was surprised by her mother's statement.

"This might not be such a bad thing. Why didn't I think of it before? It's so simple," Mom whispered.

"What are you talking about?" Priscilla asked.

"How could Mrs. Maven eating our tart be a good thing?" Penelope asked.

Mom fell back on her heals and began to explain. "Well, the snozzleberry is a pleasant memories fruit that induces a temporary state of happiness associated with pleasant memories. Theoretically, if Mrs. Maven eats even the smallest bite of the tart, she will become surrounded by the feelings and memories associated with the happiest time in her life."

"That all sounds good, but how would that help us?" Priscilla inquired.

"The snozzleberry experience can be very intense. Intense enough to soften someone like Mrs. Maven. Then we wouldn't have to perform the spell."

"But what about the fact that the snozzleberries aren't ripe yet?" Penelope asked. "You said it yourself, the unripened snozzleberries can be dangerous."

"You're right—I did say that. For the average person, consuming unripened snozzleberries can be dangerous. But, something tells me that Mrs. Maven is *not* an average person. The worst that can happen is that she will be locked in her pleasant memories forever."

"That doesn't sound too bad."

"But what about the spell?" Priscilla whined. "I wanted to do the spell."

Mom turned to her daughter and said calmly, "Sometimes fate will dictate what is to be done. It seems that this time, the matter has been taken out of our hands. There's nothing for us to do but sit back and watch."

Penelope cracked the door a little bit wider and they all peered into the kitchen.

Mrs. Maven was salivating and breathing heavily as she tore off a large piece of the tart and stuffed it into her mouth. As crumbs fell to the floor, she started to moan happily. "This tart is so good. I have to have another piece," she said, tearing off a bigger piece.

Mom turned pale. "This is not good. I did not anticipate this. A small piece would have been more than enough to induce the pleasant memories."

"What's going to happen?" Penelope asked as she forced the door open a little wider.

"Don't do that! She'll see us," Priscilla said as she leaned over and gave her sister a shove. This caused Penelope to lose her balance and fall backwards into the shelf, causing the crystal jar to fall to the floor and explode.

"**KABOOM!**" The force of the explosion blew the pantry door from its hinges and sent Penelope, Priscilla, and their mother flying across the kitchen.

When Penelope regained consciousness a few moments later, all that she could see were sparkling crystals raining down upon her. As the crystals gently floated to the floor, she put out her hand and caught some. In her hand, the crystals felt warm, like sun kissed grains of sand.

"Mom, Priscilla—are you both okay?" she called out into the crystal storm.

Mom called back, "I think we're all right. It's hard to see anything."

Penelope could tell from her mother's voice that she was near the back door. She tried to stand up. "I'm coming over to you," she said.

The crystal dust was beginning to clear and she could see her mother and sister lying on the floor near the back door. Kneeling next to them, she saw that Priscilla was unharmed, and that her mother's nostrils were flaring. "I'm so sorry, Mom!"

Sitting up, Mom ignored her daughter's attempt to apologize and glanced over towards the kitchen door.

"What do you think happened to her?" Penelope asked.

Mom's expression was one of fear. "I don't know," she replied as she stood up and stumbled towards the foyer. "We have to find her."

"Let's go!" Penelope said, grabbing the book.

Mom led the girls outside and across the street. Mrs. Maven's front door was wide open. Quietly, the three crept up the porch steps. Standing outside the front door, Penelope started to think about Pumpkin and what they did to him. "What are we going to do?" she asked.

Mom slowly lifted her hand and gently knocked on the door.

"Are you crazy? Why can't we just peek in the windows? I've found it to be very effective," said Penelope.

Mom did not say a word. A few minutes went by, as the three stood out on the cold porch. The wind was picking up, and there was a hint of snow in the air. Mrs. Maven finally came to the door. Penelope immediately noticed that she looked different. She was smiling, and her hair and clothes were clean and neat.

"May I help you," she asked sweetly?

Mom made up some excuse about wanting to know if she would buy a town raffle ticket. When Mrs. Maven went to get her purse, they all ran back to the house.

Once inside their house, the girls demanded to know what had happened to Mrs. Maven.

"She doesn't even know us," said Penelope.

"Does she remember anything?" asked Priscilla.

"Well—I think that things worked as I had hoped. Mrs. Maven's pleasant disposition seems to be a result of her living in her most pleasant memory," Mom replied as she dropped down onto the parlor sofa.

"But how long will she be this way?" Penelope asked.

Mom wasn't sure exactly, but judging by the quantity of tart she ate, she estimated it would be a very long time.

"But what about the meeting?" Priscilla asked. "In a half-hour, the townspeople are due to arrive across the street."

Mom didn't seem too concerned. "Girls, I have a plan!" she announced. "Come with me into the kitchen. The girls followed Mom into the kitchen and returned to the foyer five minutes later with a small poster, which read:

IF YOU HAVE COME FOR THE MEETING, I AM SORRY TO INFORM YOU THAT YOU HAVE WASTED YOUR TIME. I AM THE ONLY MENACING FORCE IN TOWN.

MRS MAVEN

"I hope this works," Penelope said, nervously as she fumbled with the roll of masking tape.

195

"Don't worry. It'll work," said Mom. "People in town expect this kind of behavior from Mrs. Maven."

The girls nodded in agreement as they followed Mom out the front door.

Chapter Thirteen

Priscilla Learns that She's Had it All Along

*P*riscilla thought about Mrs. Maven as she walked to school with Penelope the following day. *It's hard to believe that we don't have to worry about her anymore—but what about Jasmine? Was Oswald right about her? Could it be that she doesn't remember what happened at our house? Since she wasn't in school yesterday, I couldn't find out what she remembered. Hopefully, she'll be there today.*

"I'm so glad that our sign worked," Penelope said as the two neared the school.

"Me, too! And, could you believe so many people showed up for the meeting?"

"It was crazy," Penelope replied and then stopped.

Jasmine and three other girls were standing near the front entrance to the school. They were talking, laughing, and messing with their hair. Priscilla hoped the conversation was not about them. Jasmine saw Penelope and called out a greeting, "Hey, Penelope! Come here for a minute."

Penelope nervously raised her hand and managed a wave.

"Here's our chance to find out if she remembers," Priscilla whispered.

Penelope smiled and nodded.

"Hi, Penelope. How's it going?" Jasmine said as the two approached. "I thought that you were going to call me last weekend. What happened? I was supposed to come over to color your hair."

"Uh—I'm sorry, Jasmine. Things were kind of crazy around my house this weekend. And . . . I think that I've decided against coloring my hair again. I'm going to keep my natural color," Penelope replied, playing along with the game.

"Okay, if that's what you want. I'll talk to you later."

Penelope smiled and agreed to talk to her friend at lunch.

"I'm so glad that's over with. I think that it went well," Penelope said as she and Priscilla headed into the building.

Priscilla should have felt relief too, but could only mutter an, "I guess so."

"What do you mean, 'I guess so?' What's wrong with you today? You've been acting weird all morning."

"I guess I'm not convinced that everything is going to be okay. What if Jasmine remembers, or the spell on Mrs.

Maven wears off? We need to learn to control the book, and we need to do it soon."

To Priscilla's surprise, Penelope agreed.

That evening, before dinner, the girls closed the door to the den and settled down on the leather sofa. It was the perfect time to work on their spells without interruption, as Mom was upstairs taking a bath. Priscilla was about to open the book when the doorbell rang. "Mom will get it—let's get started," she said as she opened the book.

The doorbell rang again.

"Isn't Mom taking a bath?" asked Penelope.

The doorbell rang once more before Priscilla finally got up and ran to the door. "Who is it?" she called, putting her ear up to the door.

No one answered, but she could sense that someone was there. Slowly, she unlocked the door and opened it a crack. It was Mrs. Maven. She was standing on the porch smiling, but something told Priscilla *not* to open the door all the way.

"Hello, Priscilla," Mrs. Maven said sweetly.

Priscilla opened her mouth to return the greeting, but stopped. She knew that something was terribly wrong. She studied Mrs. Maven's face and quickly realized that it was her eyes—they were like two black holes. A chill ran through her body. She didn't understand how they could change so quickly—only a couple of days ago her eyes had sparkled.

"Hello, Mrs. Maven. What can we do for you?" Priscilla finally asked, as she glanced down at the white wicker basket in the old woman's hands.

"It's a fine evening, don't you think?" said Mrs. Maven, beaming.

Priscilla smiled and nodded, but could not take her eyes off the basket. She wanted to know what lay beneath the crisp yellow and white checked cloth napkin that was draped over the opening like a canopy.

A moment later, Penelope arrived at the door to see what was keeping her sister. "Oh! Hi, Mrs. Maven," she said warmly.

"Hello, Penelope. I'm looking for Pumpkin. He's been gone for some time now and I'm worried sick," she explained.

Priscilla's mind started to race. There was definitely something wrong. The woman's tone was friendly, but her eyes were intense and her lips kept quivering. Priscilla pulled her sister towards her and whispered, "Something's wrong here—she's not supposed to remember the past."
"What should we do? We have to tell her something."

Priscilla could see that her sister was starting to panic.

"I'll take care of this," she offered and turned to Mrs. Maven. "I'm sorry, Mrs. Maven. We haven't seen Pumpkin in a few days," she said, trying not to show any emotion.

Mrs. Maven's smile quickly turned cold. "So *you* say, but *Pumpkin* tells it differently," she said as she jerked the napkin from the basket and let it fall to the floor.

Out from under a mound of shredded newspaper slithered a hideous beast. Its head was that of a cat with fiery yellow eyes, but its body was that of a snake—long and thin, and covered with coarse-looking hairs. Priscilla knew by the beast's black and orange stripes that it was Pumpkin.

"I can bite you if I want to. Your wicked spell has given me back my teeth," Pumpkin hissed as thick, yellow slime dripped from his glistening mouth.

Priscilla jumped back as Pumpkin began to slither up the wall of the basket. As he undulated, the dark, stiff-looking hairs that covered his body made a sound like a straw broom being dragged against rough cement.

Priscilla began to scream and Penelope quickly slammed the door, but this did not stop Mrs. Maven. "How dare you use your magic on *me*! *You* don't know who you're messing with. Watch out . . . you may not be the only ones who can cast spells," she cackled.

Penelope put her ear up to the door cautiously. "She's gone," she said.

"What do you think she meant by what she just said?" Priscilla asked, trembling.

"I don't know, but this is *so* bad."

"What are we going to do?"

"Is everything all right?" Mom called, frantically, as she hurried down the stairs in her bathrobe. "I heard screaming."

"Everything's okay Mom," Priscilla replied, glancing at Penelope. "I just stubbed my toe on the chair."

"Yeah—everything's okay," added Penelope.

Mom checked Priscilla's toe and after finding no bruise, went back upstairs.

"Why did you lie to Mom?"

"Because we're going to do that transformation spell and Mom can't know about it. Don't you see that this is something that we have to do on our own?"

"But look at how we messed up the spell with Pumpkin. I think Mom was right. We aren't experienced enough to do spells on our own yet."

"Don't forget about the spell we did on Oswald. It went perfectly. I know that we can do it again, and to make sure, we are going to study the book. We are going to learn everything we need to know about performing spells so we don't mess up again."

Penelope reminded her about the crystal jar. "I'll figure out something," Priscilla reassured her.

Over the next couple of days, as soon as their homework was finished, the girls read the book. Three days later, they were finished with it and even practiced a couple of simple spells. The spells were successful and they had enough confidence to move forward with their plan. While Mom was at work, the girls decided to go into town in search of the magical crystal jar.

"Come on Priscilla—we've already been down this street," Penelope whined. "I'm cold and it's getting late."

"I know, but I have a feeling that the store we're looking for is here somewhere," Priscilla replied as she scanned the buildings up and down the block.

A minute later, she lowered her head in defeat. "I guess you were right . . . it's not here," she said softly.

"You're wrong, Priscilla," Penelope said, tugging on the sleeve of her sister's coat. "**Look!**" she cried excitedly, pointing to a tiny shop on the other side of the street.

"How . . . how is this possible?" Priscilla gasped. "That store wasn't there a few minutes ago."

Nestled snugly between two larger buildings was a tiny cement-faced, freshly painted, bright red building. Over the building's large front window hung a neon sign that read, *Potions and More.*

"It seems to have appeared out of nowhere," whispered Penelope.

"I can't explain it either, but since it is there, we should go and see if they have what we need."

Together, the two quickly made their way across the street. Once inside, Priscilla knew that it was the right place—magic was in the air. The shop consisted of one enormous room divided by rows of shelving and lit by hundreds of candles placed on pedestals of various heights. Priscilla did not see anyone else shopping as she glanced around.

"I'm not sure about this place," Penelope whispered as she rubbed her hands together. "It's cold and damp like our basement, and what's with the candles . . . and that *smell?* Let's just find the jar and get out of here."

Priscilla, who did not seem bothered by the cold or the strong smell of musk coming from the back of the store, simply said, "Wait!" and began to wander down the aisle marked, *Treats for Trickery.*

As she walked slowly past dusty shelves filled with jars, white canvas sacks and metal boxes, she read the labels: *Bitter Bubble Pigs Ears, Slimy Spider Web Catch, Chewy But Sweet Lizard's Tongues.* "This place is awesome!" she announced. Penelope, who was over three aisles, made a face. "I guess it's kind of cool. If I had seen this stuff days ago, it would have disgusted me. Take this for instance," as she read from the sign above a display for crystal orbs. "See into the future or the past with the *Mystic Orb of Lennia.*" She wriggled her nose and picked up one of the smooth glass balls. "Do you think they really work?" she said throwing the ball into the air.

"Hey! What are you doing?" Priscilla snapped as she ran over to her sister and grabbed the orb. "If you break something, we'll never be able to get the jar. I only have ten dollars on me."

"All right . . . all right," Penelope said, rolling her eyes.

After wandering up and down the same aisles and not finding a single crystal jar, both girls were feeling frustrated.

"We really need some help. There *must* be someone minding the store. Let's check out the back," said Priscilla, leading the way.

They had taken only a few steps when she noticed a strangely familiar odor that seemed to come from a corner in the rear of the store. Looking in that direction, all she saw was darkness, but the smell was getting stronger.

"Penelope, it smells like something's burning. Come on . . . let's check it out," she said, pulling her sister by the arm.

As the girls neared the dark corner, Priscilla could now see the outline of what appeared to be a table. It was as long as two yard sticks and a little wider than a picnic table bench. She also saw something she hadn't seen a minute earlier. It was the flicker of a flame.

"Priscilla, there *is* something burning over there," Penelope said, pointing at the table.

"I see it. There *must* be someone back here who can help us."

When the girls reached the table, Priscilla realized that it wasn't a table at all, but a narrow wooden desk with tiny drawers running from one end to the other. She also realized that the flame was coming from a Bunsen burner.

"I don't get it. There's no one here," she said, looking towards a doorway behind the desk, "but, maybe there's someone back *there*."

Penelope put her hands on her hips. "Sorry, sis, but I'm *not* going back there. This place is starting to creep me out."

"That's not what I was suggesting," Priscilla replied as she took notice of the articles on the desk.
In addition to the Bunsen burner, there was a black metal box, an appointment book, a calculator, a cup full of pens and an open can of soda.
"See—there must be someone here," she said pointing to the can.

Penelope sighed. "Maybe we should look up front again. This place is so big, we might have missed them when we came in," she said as she turned around and headed up one of the aisles.

Priscilla turned to follow. "Wait Penelope!" she called. "If you'd just . . ."

Priscilla stopped. There it was again, the smell of burning plastic. She glanced back over her shoulder and saw a tall thin man standing behind the desk. His hair was thick and white and his skin was brown and smooth, and he was wearing large silver-rimmed glasses. "Penelope—there's someone at the desk," she called to her sister.

"*Really?*" Penelope replied in a surprised voice, and joined her sister near the display of plastic shrunken frog heads.

The man was now standing in front of the Bunsen burner, which cast a blue light on his face. Now, for the first time since Priscilla set foot in the store, she wished that she had not.

"So that's what I smelled," she said to herself as she watched the man hold a hotdog over the blue flame with a long plastic fork.

"Let *me* handle this, Priscilla," Penelope said as she moved boldly towards the desk.

Priscilla was surprised to see her sister take control and was curious to see how she planned to handle the situation.

"Hello! I'm sorry to bother you, but we need help finding something."

As Penelope spoke, the man took a seat at the desk. I knew you'd come," he said, without looking up as he continued to turn his food over the flame.

"*How* did he know?" Penelope whispered uneasily.

"I don't know," Priscilla whispered back, afraid the man would hear them.

Suddenly, the man spoke again, but his voice was gruffer than before. "You'll find what you need over there." As he spoke, he pointed in the direction of the store's back wall, which was shrouded in darkness.

Penelope could feel her mouth start to open. "How did you know?" she heard herself ask.

With that, the man put down his fork and glanced up for only a second, but the look in his eyes let them know they had been dismissed.

"Well, thanks," Penelope said as the pair retreated in the direction the man had indicated. Then, turning to Priscilla, she asked, "Did you see his eyes?"

"Yeah—I've never seen lilac-colored eyes with blue flecks in them before. They were the strangest eyes I've ever seen."

"Hey! Didn't we come this way before? And I know we didn't see any crystal jars," Penelope said as they crept along.

"You're probably right. I think we covered every inch of this store. I just don't remember it being this dark," Priscilla said as she strained to see in front of her.

Penelope grabbed the back of her sister's coat. "Don't go too fast."

There were no candles or light of any kind in this seemingly forgotten area of the store. Feeling a little off balance, Priscilla put her hands out to her sides. When she did this, she brushed something cool and hard with her left hand. "Penelope—I feel something," she said and stopped.

"What is it?"

As if to allow Penelope to see for herself, a single light bulb, dangling from the ceiling above their heads, turned on and illuminated dozens of cut crystal jars lining a long shelf along the wall. Acting as a choreographer, the bulb directed its beam of light through the jars like sunlight through a prism causing hundreds of tiny lights to dance on the walls, up onto the ceiling, and across the floor, shattering the darkness.

"I can't believe this. How did *that* happen?" Penelope whispered.

"I have no idea. I never thought there'd be so many of them. Didn't Mom say that she bought the last one?"

"Let's just pick one and get out of here," Penelope cried.

Priscilla grabbed a crystal jar that looked like the one that Mom had brought home.

"Great! Let's pay for it and get out of here. I've seen enough of this place."

Priscilla agreed and they moved quickly to the desk to pay for the jar, but the man was gone.

"Excuse me, sir. We'd like to pay for our jar," Penelope called out.

But, no one answered and no one came.

"Why don't we just take it and get out of here," Penelope suggested.

As if in response, a gust of wind seemed to come from the doorway behind the desk and pushed them to the front of the store.

"What was *that*?" Priscilla asked as she held the enchanted crystal jar close to her.

"I don't know, but I think that means we're supposed to go now," Penelope said as she pulled open the front door. Priscilla did not say a word. She looked around the store one last time and then followed her sister out of the store.

Outside, the air had grown colder and Priscilla did not have her gloves. She placed the glass jar in her backpack where it would be safe. This allowed her to put her hands in her pockets to warm them.

"We'd better hurry home . . . it's starting to freeze out here," she said.

"You're right—Mom will be home soon. All of this took longer than I thought. Let's take the woods—it's quicker," Penelope replied, bobbing up and down.

Priscilla knew that her sister was right, but she had a strange feeling that they should stay out of the woods that day. As the wind kicked up and the air grew even more frigid, she shoved her hands into her pockets—she hated being cold. "I agree—let's take the woods home," she said, ignoring her instincts.

Nelson Woods was not far from the store. At the edge of the woods, Priscilla stopped and looked behind her. "What's wrong?" asked Penelope.

"I don't know . . . I feel like someone's following us."

Penelope looked around. "Come on, there's no one there—let's get go . . ."

But, before she could finish her sentence, some unknown force, like the strong pull of a giant magnet, drew them into the woods. **"Eeeyyyhhh!"** the girls screamed as they were lifted off the ground and carried through the air like paper dolls floating on a breeze.

Moments later, they plunged to the hard ground.

"What was *that*?" Penelope moaned, as she tried to sit up. Her purple coat was covered with black mud, thick like molasses.

Priscilla, who was finding it difficult to move, shook her head and rubbed her ankle. "I'm not sure, but I think I twisted my ankle," she replied, wincing in pain.

With much effort, Penelope managed to help her sister to her feet.

"I don't like this at all," Priscilla said, looking around. "I'm getting that feeling again. Something isn't right."

"I know what you mean—wind doesn't just pick people up and carry them through the air."

"How's the jar?" Penelope asked pointing to the backpack that was still lying on the ground.

Priscilla sighed. "I bet it's broken," she said as she bent over and carefully picked up the backpack.

She didn't need to say a word—the jingling of the broken pieces at the bottom of the bag said it all.

"Now what are we going to do?" Penelope whined.

"Get another one," Priscilla replied matter-of-factly as she slung the backpack over her shoulder. "But, not today. We have to get home."

Glancing around the woods, Priscilla noticed that there were other aspects of the woods that seemed different. Nelson Woods, which was usually a very quiet place in winter, was alive with the chatter of birds. As she looked up at the trees she wondered where they were. She could see nothing but empty tree branches and squirrel's nests.

"The woods feel so peaceful today," Penelope announced suddenly.

"Don't you hear the birds?" Priscilla asked, as she tried to put some weight on her leg.

"I don't know what you're talking . . ." Penelope began to reply.

Before she could finish her sentence, Priscilla let out a cry. "Ooooh—that hurts! Penelope—can you please help me?"

"Lean on me," Penelope said as she grabbed her sister around the waist, and Priscilla swung her arm over her sister's shoulder. "We'll be home soon."

The two clumsily navigated around the patches of mud and thick yellow moss that seemed to be everywhere by trying to walk on the clumps of withered leaves and twigs that were scattered about the ground. Priscilla could still hear the birds. Their chatter was becoming louder. "Stop for a minute!" she said as they passed by a giant old oak tree.

"What's wrong now?" Penelope asked, annoyed.

"Do you hear the birds now? They're chirping so loud—they sound as if they're right over our heads. They sound so sad," Priscilla said, frowning.

"Priscilla . . . I'm starting to worry about you. Did you hit your head back there?"

Priscilla was frustrated because she was the only one who could hear the birds. "*No,* I did not hit my head!" she replied, anger rising in her voice. "And, *I'm not hearing things!*"
"Let's take a break—I think you need one," Penelope said as she led her sister back to the old tree.

Peering up at the tree again, Priscilla realized that she no longer heard the birds. "They've stopped," she said as she ran her fingers over the tree's rough, etched bark.

Penelope sat down on a large fallen tree branch. "What time is it?" she mumbled.
Priscilla glanced at her watch. "Oh, no! It's almost four. Mom's probably home by now . . . she's going to be worried about us. We'd better go."

Without regard for the pain in her ankle, she was about to take a step when she noticed something out of the corner of her eye. A strange looking bird was perched in the dogwood tree next to the old oak. The bird was as big as a well-fed cat and as black as coal. Priscilla did not say a word, but nudged her sister.

The bird stretched out its wings and flew over to the old oak. It landed on a branch directly above them.

"Was that the bird that you heard?" Penelope asked timidly.

"I'm not sure."

Penelope grabbed Priscilla and tried to run, but Priscilla quickly fell to the muddy ground. Penelope stopped and pulled her to her feet. "Look at me—thanks a lot Penelope!" Priscilla wailed as she shook the mud from her jacket.

Penelope, whose eyes had become as big as tennis balls, said nothing.

"**What's wrong with you?**" Priscilla shouted.

Penelope, who was now trembling, pointed over Priscilla's left shoulder.

Priscilla turned around to see a figure dressed all in black standing behind her.

"**WHERE ARE YOU RUSHING OFF TO?**" the figure asked in a powerful voice that echoed through the trees.

Priscilla thought there was something familiar about the voice.

Frightened, Penelope grabbed her arm. "What do we do?"

Priscilla's first impulse was to grab her sister's arm and flee, but she knew it would be futile. She tried to move her legs, but something held them firm to the ground. *Stay and fight*, a little voice inside her said.

"Who are you?" Priscilla asked, trying to keep her lip from quivering.

The figure floated menacingly towards her and removed its hood with its long bony fingers. As it did, Priscilla noticed a tattoo on the figure's forearm. She recognized it immediately as being the same tattoo she saw on Mrs. Willowby's arm. Priscilla wondered how Mrs. Willowby could possibly be connected to this monster.

With the hood removed, she saw it was an old woman with long silvery hair and wide scarlet eyes. As Priscilla tried to turn her eyes away, the woman started to laugh.

Priscilla watched the woman's mouth as it moved and contorted. Then it hit her—the woman was Mrs. Maven. She recognized the way the lines around her mouth turned upward when she laughed. *I can't believe it*, she thought. *Mrs. Maven is a witch with strong powers.*

Over to her side, Penelope began to whimper. "Priscilla—I'm afraid!"

Priscilla became angry. She was tired of Mrs. Maven interfering in their lives. She had to end this now, but how? Before she could think, she found her hand unzipping her backpack, which was slung over her shoulder.

Mrs. Maven, who had been watching Priscilla closely, cackled, "You must learn to trust yourself. That is the first rule that an Enlightened One must learn."

Priscilla remembered that her grandmother had said the exact same thing. "I know who you are—what do you know about the Enlightened Ones?" she asked, letting go of the zipper.

"Not nearly enough, but I know plenty about you."

"What are you talking about?" Priscilla asked as she watched Mrs. Maven pull her hood back over her head.

"What is she doing?" Penelope whispered.
"I don't know."

Suddenly the old woman began to speak in a familiar voice, but a voice that was not her own. "I'd tell Penelope a thing or two about how she's changed and how much I hate her new look. I'd also tell her what phonies I think her friends are."

When Mrs. Maven finished speaking, the woods became as still as a winter's night. Penelope and Priscilla looked at each other with expressions of both shock and fear. After a few moments, Penelope's eyes became full of tears. "Please tell me what's going on here. How did she do that Priscilla? That was your voice coming from her mouth."

Priscilla searched for the right words to tell her sister how much she regretted her hurtful thoughts. "I'm sorry Penelope," was all she could manage.

"So it's true . . . that's how you really feel about me?"

Priscilla lowered her head. She could no longer look at her sister. She felt ashamed of what she had said in anger. But she was also furious with Mrs. Maven for hurting her sister.

"**Ha ha ha ha hee**," Mrs. Maven cackled like a cheap Halloween decoration. "I cannot believe that I am standing before the *two* who would follow in the footsteps of *Abisius* himself. I see no power *here*."

The girls looked at each other.

"She's right Priscilla. We are pathetic. We can't even be honest with each other."

"I'm sorry that I didn't tell you, but I didn't want to get into another fight. Things hadn't exactly been cozy between us for a long time, but there's been a change for the better lately—I didn't want to ruin it."

"I guess you're right . . . but what do we do now?"

"I'll tell you what you should do," screeched Mrs. Maven. "You should hand the book over to me and go on home like good little witches."

Priscilla hugged the backpack. "**Never!**" she yelled defiantly.

"**Then, I will take it!**" Mrs. Maven shouted and cast a glowing orange ball of fire in their direction.

Penelope screamed as the fireball missed her head and struck a nearby tree. Instantly, the tree burst into flame and then disintegrated into a pile of gray ash.

"All right—if that's how you want to play—we can play rough too," said Priscilla, reaching into her backpack. She could feel the book underneath the sharp shards of glass from the broken crystal jar. She could also feel the soft body of Sarah's doll, which she had forgotten about.

Suddenly the book started to move on its own and quickly sprang out to touch the cold winter air. Before Priscilla could catch it, Mrs. Maven drew it to her like a screw to a magnet. **"Give it back to us!"** Priscilla demanded. **"That's our book!"**

Mrs. Maven laughed as the book jumped into her hands. "That's where you're wrong. This book belongs to me. I've waited many years to claim it for myself," she said, holding the book tightly against her chest.

"You're crazy!" shouted Penelope. **"Our grandmother gave the enchanted book to us!"**

Mrs. Maven explained how Abisius gave the book to her great, great-grandmother. "This book was supposed to be mine. With it, I will be the most powerful Enlightened One to have ever existed," she said, running her fingers gently over the book's cover.

"Is the book the reason why you've been harassing and threatening us all this time?" Priscilla asked.

"For many years I had hoped to meet another one of our kind, who would have information about the whereabouts of the book. Then something unexpected happened—your family moved here. I knew from the moment I set eyes on you, that you and I were alike. When the house changed, I knew that it was the work of magic. With the help of Pumpkin and Relleck, I discovered that you had the book."

"Relleck?" Priscilla asked.

Mrs. Maven began to cackle uncontrollably and lifted her long wrinkled arm and pointed to the sky. Priscilla followed the woman's movement with her eyes to a point just above the treetops.

"I don't see anything," whimpered Penelope. "What is she up to now?"

"Shh!" snapped Priscilla. "I hear something."

"I think I hear it too . . . it sounds like a flock of birds. Is that what you heard before?"

"Yes," said Priscilla. "But now they sound different—stronger."

Before another word could be spoken, a flock of large gray birds were finally visible overhead. As they soared down towards them, Priscilla realized that her bird, Tikki, was part of the group. "*Tikki?*" she asked as she watched the birds land in the trees around them.

Tikki did not follow the others, but landed on Mrs. Maven's shoulder.

"Hello, Relleck," she greeted the bird fondly. "I'm glad that you and your friends decided to join our little party." Relleck did not speak words like Mrs. Maven's other followers, but chirped strongly and ruffled her feathers, which had darkened to a royal blue. Mrs. Maven seemed to understand the bird and replied, "We will have it soon enough."

"What is *Tikki* doing with *her*? She's our bird," Penelope whispered.

"**She never belonged to you,**" Mrs. Maven shrieked. "**Relleck belongs to no one.**"

"**Then why did you give her to me?**" Priscilla shouted.

Mrs. Maven smiled cruelly. "To spy, of course. Pumpkin could only get so close. I needed to know your inner thoughts."

"**You're sick!**" shouted Penelope.

"You're not so innocent yourself," replied Mrs. Maven. "Was it not you and your sister who turned my baby, Pumpkin, into a hideous beast and me into a happy fool? I bet you're wondering how I got out of that one."

The girls nodded.

"The day that you so carelessly left the enchanted book alone, Relleck took the opportunity to obtain the missing parts to some spells, including the reversal spell to *The Enchanted Snozzleberry Tart recipe*."

"I wondered why her cage was open," Priscilla said to herself.

"After Pumpkin disappeared, Relleck was even more valuable to me."

Priscilla put her arm around her sister. "We were only trying to protect ourselves against you. You've been threatening our family ever since we moved here."

Mrs. Maven floated over to the girls. "So, I guess we're not so different. I need this book to protect myself."

The thought of being anything like Mrs. Maven was almost too much for Priscilla to bear. "The only thing that we have in common is being part of the same past, and that's as far as it goes. The Enlightened Ones that my grandmother told me about used their magic for good," she replied, shaking her fist. "I know about how you tried to use magic to take over the town."

"ENOUGH!" Mrs. Maven commanded as a fierce wind began to whip up around them. She held the book in one hand and reached into the pocket of her robe with the other.

"Oswald!" shouted Priscilla.

Mrs. Maven was holding her friend up by his jacket collar.

"You leave him alone, or I'll . . ."

"You'll *what*? What could *you* possibly do? I have the book now."

Something inside Priscilla snapped, and she could think of nothing but helping her friend. She grabbed a large tree branch from the ground and began to hobble towards the old woman; the pain in her ankle was nothing compared to the thought of losing her friend. "**Let my friend go!**" she screamed as she raced forward.

With that, Mrs. Maven raised her arms up over her head and began to chant. As she did, both the book and Oswald fell to the ground. Oswald scurried away as fast as he could. When Priscilla saw that her friend was okay, she stopped.

Since Mrs. Maven was preoccupied and making no attempt to retrieve the book, Priscilla decided to take this opportunity to grab it.

In a blink of an eye, Mrs. Maven bent down and snatched the book off the ground.

"**HA HA HA HA HA**," she laughed so loud that the ground shook. Then, reaching into her pocket once more, she grabbed a fistful of a pale green powder and threw it at Priscilla. Lying on the ground, covered in green dust, Priscilla was unable to move a muscle. Mrs. Maven began to chant:

"From here to there . . . from this to that . . . I change you witch into a mangy rat.

Poof! A cloud of green smoke surrounded Priscilla like a wall. When the smoke cleared, she had been transformed into a small white rat.

"**NO!**" Penelope screamed, with tears in her eyes. She ran over to her sister and knelt down next to her. "Priscilla—what has she done to you? I'm so sorry! I should have done something to help. If I had been a better sister, then maybe this wouldn't have happened."

Penelope wiped her face and looked up at Mrs. Maven. **"Change her back!"** she demanded.

Mrs. Maven laughed and told her that if she had taken the magic seriously, none of this would have happened.

Penelope began to whimper.

All of a sudden, like morning mist rising off a lake, Mrs. Willowby appeared. **"Change her back right now!"** she demanded.

The lines on Mrs. Maven's face softened the moment she set eyes on Mrs. Willowby. "It can't be," she said. "Is that you, my old friend?"

"Maybe once—a long time ago. Let the girls go . . . they mean you no harm. They are young and inexperienced."

Priscilla, who could still see and hear everything that was happening, twitched. She was shocked to know that the two had once been friends.

"Not so inexperienced that they turned my cat into a snake beast, and cast a spell on me, too."

"They were only trying to protect themselves in the same way that you have done for all these years," Mrs. Willowby said as she made her way over to where Mrs. Maven was standing.

Mrs. Maven did not respond.

"That book doesn't belong to you, Delilah. Your grandmother was supposed to hand it down to you, but once she saw how evil you had become . . ." she continued, pointing to the book.

"Either you give it to me, or I'll take it myself. You know that I can . . . I did it once before when you stole it."

Penelope gasped. "Mrs. Maven's the one that Grandma told us about—the one who stole the enchanted book," she said.

"**The book belongs to me now, Laurel!**" shrieked Mrs. Maven. "I'll change back the girl if you wish, but the book is mine."

Mrs. Willowby sighed. "I'm afraid that I'm not in a bargaining mood," she said, raising her arms over her head.

The sky overhead turned dark as night and the stars shone brightly in the sky. The air grew bitterly cold and Penelope held Priscilla closer.

"The winds of time sweep at our feet . . . our hands they hold on tightly . . . take away the night . . . and the beast too . . . give back the day . . . and return the girl to her natural state," Mrs. Willowby chanted.

The book broke free from Mrs. Maven's grasp and jumped into Mrs. Willowby's arms. The wind that had been blowing steadily, bringing cold air with it, grew still. So still, that it felt as if the air was being sucked away.

Priscilla could hardly breathe. She wondered if, for an instant, time had actually stopped. She closed her eyes. When she opened them a second later, she saw that daylight had returned and she had been changed back. Gazing up into Penelope's red and teary face, she felt safe. "I'm all right," she said and took a deep breath.

The air returned, and brought with it a new sense of calm. Penelope began to cry. "I'm so glad you're back, Priscilla. I'm so sorry for not being there for you lately," she wailed. "It's just that ever since Dad died, I haven't felt like myself. I've had these feelings—like something inside me was missing."

Priscilla nodded and grabbed Penelope's hand.

"I guess I thought that if I changed myself, I would feel better again. Can you ever forgive me?"

Priscilla tried to sit up. "It's okay—I'm glad that you finally told me," she said. "Just promise me that you'll never shut me out again. You have to learn to trust in the people who love you."

Penelope promised to never forget what she had learned, and the two hugged. When they moved apart, they realized that Mrs. Maven and Mrs. Willowby were arguing. Priscilla saw that Mrs. Willowby was holding the book, and she knew that she had to get it back. But before she could make a move, the book struggled free from Mrs. Willowby's grasp and flew into her arms.

"Tis how it *should* be," Mrs. Willowby shouted.

"Let's get out of here," Penelope said as she took hold of Priscilla's arm.

"No, wait! We have to help Mrs. Willowby!" Priscilla shouted, pushing her sister away.

Penelope looked confused. "I'd love to help her, but what can *we* do?"

Priscilla thought for a minute. She looked down at the book. "Trust in the magic . . . the magic is the key—but, maybe the book is the key, too," she said to herself. "What did you say?"

Priscilla did not answer, and Mrs. Willowby called to them.

"The doll," she said. "It couldn't save Sarah, but . . . ."

Priscilla immediately reached into her backpack and pulled out the doll.

"I didn't know that you brought it," Penelope said. "What are you going to do?"

"I don't know, yet."

Priscilla was quiet for a moment, but she could still hear Mrs. Willowby and Mrs. Maven arguing. "Penelope, I need you to trust me—I think I have an idea."

Penelope indicated that she would do anything that her sister wanted.

"This doll must have a lot of power, or Maggie wouldn't have helped me find it. I have a feeling that the power lies in the band of jewels."

"I hope you're right."

Priscilla quickly came up with a plan and explained it to her sister. Holding the doll in the air, Priscilla shouted, **"Maven . . . look what I have!"**

Mrs. Maven turned around. "Abisius," she said, her eyes as big and red as hot coals. "How did you get the sacred doll?"

"*How* is not important. What *is* important is that with this doll and the book, my sister and I will be more powerful than you ever were or could be."

Looking over at Mrs. Willowby, who was holding her walking stick in the air, Priscilla felt assured that she was doing the right thing.

"You stupid little girl—you could never be more powerful than me," Mrs. Maven howled as she flew towards Priscilla.

"Come on Penelope," Priscilla shouted as she hobbled towards Fisherman's Friend Pond. The small pond, which had been frozen solid for weeks, was mostly thawed. Standing at the water's edge, Priscilla yelled again, **"Hey, Maven!"** She held up the doll and the book.

But the old woman was nowhere to be found.

"Where do you think she went?" Penelope asked looking around.

"I'm not sure," said Priscilla as she turned to face the pond.

Then, turning back around to scan the woods, she found herself looking straight into her father's eyes. For a moment she stood there trembling.

"How can this be?" she mumbled in disbelief.

"Dad?" Penelope cried as she joined her sister.

The tall, blonde-haired, brown-eyed man was dressed in a fine navy blue suit and red tie.

"Dad?" Priscilla asked, moving closer.

Penelope had tears in her eyes. "Dad, is that really you?"

The man did not answer, but only smiled at the girls.

Priscilla could not believe her eyes, and turned them away. She glanced down at the doll in her hands. "The little old man's smile had somehow turned into a scowl. None of this is real," she said to herself. "Penelope, he's not our dad!"

"How do you know?"

"Trust me," Priscilla said as she grabbed her sister's arm. "Move away."

As the girls backed away, the image of their father began to melt into the dirt like an ice statue in the blazing sun.

"I've had enough of your tricks Maven," Priscilla screamed as she looked around. **"Show yourself, and let's finish this!"**

Mrs. Willowby, who was now leaning against a tree, smiled at Priscilla and gave a nod. The gesture, which Priscilla perceived to be a sign of approval, gave her more confidence.

"What's it gonna be, Maven?" she shouted, holding up the doll.

Mrs. Maven appeared like the sun from behind the clouds. "I, too, am ready to finish it," she said soaring from the path over to the pond like a bird about to snatch its prey. **"I would have thought that you learned your lesson?"** she shrieked, as she raised her arms and squinted her eyes, which were now on fire.

Priscilla felt the book and doll pulling away from her. She couldn't let Mrs. Maven have them. She tightened her grip. **"Don't try to fight me little girl—you are not as strong as you think,"** shrieked Mrs. Maven.

Priscilla felt herself let go of the book. "You must learn to trust in yourself," Mrs. Maven had said earlier, and the words now rang in her head. With all of her strength, she tightened her grip on the book and the doll, and stood up tall.

"You're wrong about me, Mrs. Maven. I *am* as strong as I think I am, and as smart, too," she said, casting the book out onto the pond.

Mrs. Maven tried to draw it to her, but could not. **"You may have done something to block my magic, but I'm still going to have my book back!"** she shouted. **"And the doll, too!"**

Mrs. Maven soared out over the pond. Floating above the thin layer of ice that coated the surface, she extended her arm and tried to draw the book to her once more. The book did not move. "If it will not come to me, I will go to it," she said as she lowered herself onto the ice.

Snap . . . pop . . . crack! Instantly, the ice began to break apart. Priscilla watched as Mrs. Maven's body faded into the fog hanging over the pond. "You're not as smart as you think!" Priscilla heard her say.

As her words faded away, they were replaced by a loud *HISSSS* like that of a hot poker being plunged into ice water.

"She's gone!" Priscilla announced, waving away the gray smoke that had wafted over from the pond. For a second, she could feel Mrs. Maven all around her.

"What do you think happened to her?" Penelope asked as she neared the edge of the pond.

"I'm hoping that she went somewhere far away from here. A place where she won't be able to use her powers to hurt people," Priscilla replied as she turned around towards the pond. **"Oh, NO! The book!"**

The book, which was still lying on the ice, was starting to sink. But, before Priscilla could move, it rose up through the smoke and floated back into her arms as if it were being reeled in on a fishing pole.

Priscilla turned around to see Penelope and Mrs. Willowby standing together behind her. "What do you think happened to her, Mrs. Willowby?" she asked as she peered out over the pond.

Mrs. Willowby sighed. "I wish I knew the answer to that," she replied, smiling sweetly. "I cared about her so much at one time."

Priscilla looked into Mrs. Willowby's eyes. "Are you one of us, too?" she asked.

"Yes! Delilah and I were best friends at one time. When we were very young, she was different—kind and gentle."

"Was that when you got the tattoos?"

"Yes, a long time ago, in our culture, friends and family members marked themselves to show affection and loyalty."

Mrs. Willowby's head dropped forward and Priscilla could barely hear her when she muttered, "I wish that I knew what caused Delilah to use her power for evil."

Priscilla did not know what to say. She glanced over at her sister and mouthed the words, "Say something."

"Uh . . . Priscilla—what you did was so amazing," she said, smiling warmly at her sister.

Priscilla was glad that her sister understood.

"Yeah . . . it was, wasn't it—and brave too, if I do say so myself," Priscilla announced proudly. "It was as if something inside me was giving me the courage to face Mrs. Maven."

"It's called self-confidence," said Mrs. Willowby. "You've shown signs of it before."

"I guess I convinced myself that I was weak. When we moved here, I thought that it was the magic that was giving me strength. Now I know that the magic only helped me to see what was already there."

"I always knew that you were strong," said Penelope. "Remember the time when we were nine and Mom was late picking us up from school, so we decided to walk home. When a vicious dog came out from an alley, I began to scream, but you didn't panic. You grabbed a piece of wood and scared him off."

Priscilla stared at the icy pond and smiled. "Oh, yeah! I guess I forgot about that."

"But how did you know about the doll?" Penelope asked, taking the doll, whose smile had returned, from her sister.

"I had a little help from a friend," Priscilla replied, looking over to Mrs. Willowby, who appeared weaker than ever before.

"Forgive me girls, but I am old and tired," she said as she sat down on a fallen tree.

Penelope knelt down next to her. "Mrs. Willowby, I'd really like to thank you for giving my sister back to me. I never knew how much she meant to me until I almost lost her," she said with tears in her eyes.

Mrs. Willowby smiled. "It is I who should be thanking you," she said taking Penelope's hand.

She glanced at Priscilla. "Both of you, and your mother," she said.

"For what?" asked Priscilla.

"For taking care of Maggie for my family," Mrs. Willowby replied as she rose from her perch.

Penelope and Priscilla looked at each other. "Maggie belonged to *your* family?" they both asked, gasping.

"Yes, she did. I've waited so long for a family to come along who would love her and take care of her. I can see that she is very happy now. That would have made Sarah very happy."

"Are you Sarah's grandmother?" Priscilla asked.

Mrs. Willowby nodded.

"Here—you should have this," Priscilla said, handing Mrs. Willowby Sarah's doll.

Mrs. Willowby smiled. "Thank you," she said and slowly hobbled away.

When the girls got home, Priscilla was surprised to see both her mother and her grandmother standing at the front door. She immediately noticed the look of concern in her mother's eyes.

"I was so worried about the two of you!" Mom exclaimed as she hugged her girls tightly. "What happened? Why are your clothes so dirty? Where were you all this time?"

The girls told Mom and Grandma everything over dinner.

"If it were not for the magic of Sarah's doll, I don't know if I would have been able to defeat Mrs. Maven," Priscilla said.

Grandma smiled gently at Priscilla. "There's something I have to tell you dear," she said.

Priscilla waited for her grandmother to speak.

"Sarah's doll contained no more magic than this pork chop," she said, picking up the chop with her fork.

"I don't understand. Mrs. Willowby told me that the doll was very special. Did she lie?"

"No, of course she didn't. The doll was most likely given to Sarah by her grandmother, Mrs. Willowby. Of course, that would have made it very special to her. I think that Mrs. Willowby led you to believe that the doll had magical powers to give you confidence."

"But what about the others who believed in the doll and had been searching for it for years? Even Mrs. Maven believed the doll was powerful."

"I'm sorry to say that the whole story about the doll possessing magic was just that—a story."

"The good news is that *you* defeated Mrs. Maven on your own."

Priscilla smiled the biggest smile. "I can't take all of the credit. Penelope helped too, just by being there. We're a team you know."

Penelope smiled at her sister. "Don't forget about Mrs. Willowby," she said. "If it wasn't for her, you might still be twitching your nose and looking for cheese."

Everyone laughed, except for Mom.

"Don't even joke about that," she snapped. "It seems that Mrs. Maven was working with some pretty dark magic. I had no idea that such evil even existed."

"I knew from the first time I saw her that she was bad news. But it was that day in the woods when she attacked me that I was convinced she was pure evil," said Priscilla. "She had such hate in her eyes. I wonder what happened to make her that way."

"I don't know, honey," Mom replied. We may never know."

Mom stood up and headed over to Priscilla. "I am so sorry that I wasn't there to help you girls," she said. "We moved here so that you would have a better life."

"It's okay, Mom."

"Yeah, Mom! Don't worry about it," added Penelope. "I consider the whole thing to have been a great learning experience."

Mom smiled at her daughter and headed to the sink. "You know what, girls—I think we need to celebrate. What happened today was a victory for our people. With Mrs. Maven gone, we will all be able to breathe a little easier. I always knew you girls were going to be a great team. I'm glad that you found each other again."

"Thanks to you and Grandma," Penelope said, with a smile. "If it weren't for you guys, I might have done something really stupid like spend the entire summer planning my fall wardrobe."

"Great! Now you'll probably spend the summer trying to get me to wear a hot pink bikini," Priscilla said as she made a face at her sister, who made a face back.

"You know, everything that's happened since you gave us the book has showed me how foolishly I was behaving. I now know that it's what's on the inside of a person that really counts," said Penelope.

Priscilla stood up and walked over to the refrigerator. "Seriously, Penelope, I'm glad that you're back," she said as she grabbed a soda.

Mom went over and kissed each of her daughters on the top of her head. "It's good to see you both together again. I'm so proud of you both!"

That night, the girls tossed Tikki's cage into the garbage and headed to the fireplace room with the book. "I hope that we'll never be fooled like that again," Penelope said as she put the book on the floor and plopped down on the window seat.

"It was all *my* fault. I should have listened to my instincts," Priscilla said, sitting down in the rocking chair. "I had a feeling that something wasn't right when Tikki bit me."

"Yeah, you're right. You should have known," Penelope said, smiling at her sister.

"Oh, *really?*" Priscilla said and hurled a throw pillow at her. "Well . . . guess what I heard at school yesterday?"

"What?" Penelope asked, sitting up straight.

"I heard a couple of older girls talking about how 'last-season' your purple boots are," Priscilla said.

Penelope looked like she was about to cry. "Really?"

"Gotcha!" Priscilla said, smiling and put her arms up to shield her face.

"Oooo, you! Don't worry. I'm not going to do anything now. I'll wait till you're not expecting it, and I'll get you back."

For the rest of the evening, the girls took turns reading the book aloud over a bowl of popcorn and chocolate-covered marshmallows and they laughed and teased each other just like old times. Priscilla joined her sister for lunch at school every day and Penelope, who still hung out with Jasmine, invited Priscilla to join them as much as possible.

With a lot of help from Mom and Grandma, in time, the girls learned how to control the book, and they were thrilled to be able to leave it by itself, once they found a safe place for it. Penelope figured where better than their favorite place in the whole house—the fireplace room. And, what better hiding spot than under the window seat.

As summer vacation drew near, the girls looked forward to having more time to spend lying around the house, reading and trying new recipes and spells. Priscilla compromised and bought a navy blue bikini and Penelope stopped wearing her mother's bright blue eye shadow.

As for Maggie, the enchanted house, she couldn't be happier because she once again had a family to love and take care of her. And if love could be seen as rays of light, it would shine brightly from each of her windows. And at night, from towns near and far, the light could be seen as a golden halo over the small town of Dunville.

Coming Soon

Penelope and Priscilla
and the City of the Banished

Penelope and Priscilla are enjoying a trouble-free summer vacation until Penelope takes notice of a passage in the "secrets" section of the enchanted book. Even though she and her sister had read the passage once before, this time it seems to have a different meaning for her. The passage refers to an opening in the earth which leads to another world. Penelope remembers seeing a strange boarded-up hole in the floor of their tool shed and becomes curious as to what is inside. When the girls ask their mother about the hole, she becomes angry and warns them not to go near the rickety old building because it is unsafe. Unable to stop thinking about the mysterious hole, the girls eventually disobey their mother and venture into the shed. After removing the boards, they are surprised to find that the hole has disappeared.

Soon after the incident, strange and unexplainable things begin to take place in Dunville. An evil force which presents itself to Penelope in the form of a dark figure dressed in black, takes over Jasmine. Penelope also begins acting strangely after she brings forth a vision of a boy during a séance. She begins hanging out with Jasmine again, forgetting all about her family obligations. Curious as to the identity of the boy and afraid that she is once again losing her sister, Prisicilla asks for her grandmother's help. Grandma suggests that they consult someone more powerful and knowledgeable than herself.

When they find Mrs. Willowby, she tells them about a sorceress who may be able to help. The sorceress already knows about the problems with Penelope and the boy in her vision. The sorceress offers Priscilla information about an underground city and a spell that will bring her sister back. When the spell works, the girls venture down into the mysterious hole in their back yard. It is here where they finally learn the identity of the dark figure and the whereabouts of the boy. Now, they must use everything that they've learned about magic and themselves to save the boy in the vision, defeat the dark figure and protect the people of Dunville.

Jennifer Troulis

Jennifer Troulis began sculpting at the age of five, but did not stop there. As a child, she took great pleasure in using her imagination to make toys such as wood-carved marionettes, a dollhouse made from scrap wood, rag dolls, and even a ventriloquist doll. In kindergarten, her enjoyment of writing and illustrating stories based on her home life and beloved fairy tails added to her love affair with the arts. As she got older, she took a break from writing and pursued other creative outlets, including sculpting and painting.

Over the years, she has worked diligently to establish her cleaning business. She was successful, but something was missing. After giving birth to her two children, and twenty-seven years after she put down her pen, she returned to writing. If you asked her why she took such a long break from writing, she would no doubt tell you that her twins were the inspiration that she needed to wake that sleeping part of her.